THE ARRANGEMENT

AN AGE GAP, BRATVA ROMANCE

K.C. CROWNE

ALSO BY K.C. CROWNE

K.C. Crowne is an Amazon Top 8 Bestseller

All books are FREE on Kindle Unlimited and can be read as standalones.

Antonov & Nicolaevich Bratva Brothers Series

Highest Bidder | Bratva Daddy| Owned by the Bratva| Knocked Up by the Bratva| Ruthless Rival| Scarred Prince| The Closer|Brother's Best Friend|Devil's Nuptials|

Silver Fox Daddies

Doctor Daddy| Taboo Daddy| Daddy's Best Friend| Daddy's Law| My Ex Boyfriend's Dad| Daddy's Girl| My Ex-Best friend's Daughter| Secret Daddy| Christmas with Dad's Best Friend| Vegas Daddy| Daddy's Obsession| Royal Daddy | Irish King| My Ex's Dad| The Doctor Who Stole Christmas| Daddy's Orders| His Demands| The Arrangement

Mountain Men of Liberty Series

Baby for the Mountain Man| Junior for the Mountain Man| Knocked Up by the Mountain Man| Baby For Daddy's Friend | Triplets for the Mountain Man | Taken by the Mountain Man| Secret Baby for the Mountain Man | Mountain Man's Accidental Surprise | Quadruplets for the Mountain Man | Delivering His Gifts| Mountain Daddy's Fate | Mountain Man's Lucky Charm | Mountain Man's Rival | Small Town Mountain Daddy | Mountain Man's Gift| Mountain Man's Christmas Surprise| Mountain Man's Valentine| Big Daddy| Fireworks with Three Mountain Men| Faking Mr. Right

Doctors of Denver Series

Doctor's Secret | Doctor's Surprise Delivery | Irish Doctor's Secret Babies | Millionaire's Surprise Triplets | Doctor's Baby Plan| Knocked Up by the New Zealand Doctor | Doctor's Duties | Billion Dollar Mistake | Irish Doctor Gift| Irish Doctor's Orders| Irish Doctor's Valentine| Secret Babies for my Best Friend's Dad | Secret Baby Next Door| Secret Babies for the Mafia Doctor| Secret Babies for my Dad's Best Friend|

Checkout KC's full Amazon Catalog

All books are FREE on Kindle Unlimited and can be read as standalones.

DESCRIPTION

He's old enough to be my father.
He might have killed my boyfriend.
And his scandalous offer leaves me speechless.

Not only is my boyfriend dead, he left me with a sizable loan in my name.
So an intimidating Russian mobster arrives at my door.
He proposes an unthinkable arrangement: ***repay him with my body***.
I immediately reject his offer ... but the indecent proposal haunts me for days.
In the privacy of my bed...
The handsome silver fox dominates my thoughts.
I touch myself gently and scream his name in abandon.
A knock at the door startles me.
It's Maksim.
He bugged my apartment.

And now he's here to claim what we both desperately need.

Dive into a full-length standalone romance featuring a single dad, older man, bratva enforcer within the notorious bestselling Silver Fox Daddies series. Be sure to have a cool glass of water handy—the heat level is off the charts! K.C. Crowne is an Amazon Top 6 Bestseller and an International Bestselling Author.

CHAPTER 1

TORY

"Earth to Tory," Ty, my coworker and best friend jokes, his fingers snapping me back to the present. I meet his gaze, and he softens.

"Sorry," I reply, shaking my head and trying my best to snap out of the fog. "Just... you know."

"It's fine, girl," he says. "One minute you're at a funeral, the next you're giving a golden doodle his flea meds. You're more than entitled to be a little out of it." He leans on the counter, his eyes heavy with concern.

In the dim light of the cold afternoon, Paws and Play, the pet daycare I've poured my heart and soul into feels more like a sanctuary than a business. I'm barely keeping my head above water—not because of grief of my ex's death, but from the sheer weight of reality crashing down on me.

Ned's gone. The man who once whispered sweet nothings, promising the world as we lay together, only to use those same lips to lie and manipulate, has left this earth with a finality that's as unexpected as a Siberian winter in July.

They said it was a heart attack, but he was only thirty. Who would have thought that a man who lived on the edge, who dabbled in the murky waters of the Russian mafia, would go out not with a bang, but with a whimper? The irony isn't lost on me. Ned, with his devil-may-care smile and a penchant for danger, always seemed invincible. Apparently, he wasn't.

Ty leans closer. "How are you holding up, all things considered?"

I let out a deep sigh, feeling the weight of his question. "I'm conflicted. Shouldn't I be more upset? It's not every day someone close to you dies."

Ty playfully scoffs. "Close? Please, Ned was dead weight—figuratively and now literally. Trust me, you're better off without that kind of drag in your life." His tone is light, an attempt to chase away the shadows with his wit.

A laugh bursts from me, surprising even myself. "That's awful," I reply, but I can't deny the truth in his joke, or the way it makes the corners of my lips twitch up.

"And can we talk about your funeral chic?" he goes on, his eyes twinkling as he takes in my attire. "Going straight from a graveside service to work and still managing to be the most stylish one in Wicker Park—it should be illegal."

I find myself smiling, genuinely this time, looking down at the funeral dress I hadn't had the time to change out of, my work apron on top of it. The absurdity of it all isn't lost on me; here I am, wearing my grief like a well-tailored garment to my day job because life refuses to stand still, even for a moment, even for death.

"Instead of going from the day to night look, it's the funeral to work look," I shoot back. "I'm a trend setter."

Ty laughs. He isn't just the only other worker in this place, he's also my best friend, my anchor in the stormy sea that is my life. With his striking green eyes and a style that cuts through the mundane, he's more than just help; he's my lifeline. Amid barks and messes, his humor and unwavering support are what keep me grounded.

Ty and I shuffle around the cluttered space, our dream teetering on the edge of both reality and ruin. We're *finally* starting to see a sliver of profit, a flicker of success in a venture that has consumed every ounce of our energy.

"I looked over the books for the last month today and can you believe it? We're actually not drowning in red for once," I say, pouring water into a bowl for a sprightly beagle named Benny, his tail a wagging blur of excitement.

Ty, busy untangling a leash from around a golden retriever named Lucy's legs, grins. "Just barely. But hey, from red to black is a journey, right? Next stop, green!"

"How are we supposed to turn this into a real moneymaker, though?" I sigh, watching Benny lap up the water with gusto.

"Stay positive, Tory. We've got some loyal regulars. That's more than most can say at this stage," Ty counters. Ty gives me a nudge, his tone taking on a conspiratorial bent. "Speaking of money," he says nodding toward the window, "check out Mr. Richy-rich mystery man outside. Nothing like a little eye candy to distract you from your ex's untimely demise."

"*Ty!*"

I follow his gaze to find a man seated on the bench across the street from the shop, right in front of the park entrance. He's striking in a way that halts your breath—a rugged ensemble of broad shoulders and a powerful physique. His hair is salt and pepper, his suit dark and perfectly fitted. He sits with total composure and confidence, one arm draped over the back of the bench, his gaze up and away, as if he's got something serious on his mind. He's older, too – likely in his mid-forties.

"He's... interesting," I admit, though my voice is filled with caution. "But the last thing I need right now is to complicate my life any more than it already is."

Ty chuckles, turning his attention back to Lucy. "Girl, who said anything about complicating? I'm talking about a little harmless fun. You know, the kind where you don't call him back the next day. And the guy's *clearly* loaded."

"How can you tell?"

"The suit – that's bespoke all the way. And I'd recognize a Patek-Phillipe from across the city."

Men with money has never been something that attracts my attention, and the man across the street is no exception. Something else draws me to him, though, something I can't quite put my finger on.

"What's he even doing there, anyway?" I ask.

Ty shrugs. "Probably just enjoying the view. Not illegal to sit on a bench, you know."

The man is a total enigma. Handsome, yes, but with a strange, serious air about him I can sense even from a distance. My heart tugs with curiosity, yet my mind is firm—there's no room for distractions, especially not of the male variety.

Ty glances at his watch, a not-so subtle hint that he's ready to be done for the day. "Looks like it's about closing time," he says. "Got my evening stuff done. Need me to stay and help wrap things up? I can totally understand if you're not in the mood to do the books for tonight."

I shake my head, exhaustion pulling at me. All I want to do is go to bed and sleep. "No, you go ahead. You've done more than enough today. Seriously – over and above the call of duty."

He pauses, his smile flickering with a hint of concern. "Sure? How about you come out with me and the gang for drinks? Might do you some good to unwind a bit."

The offer tempts me for a fleeting moment—the promise of laughter and distraction. But fatigue, both physical and emotional, claims victory. "I'm just too tired. I'd be a total Debbie Downer. But thanks. As soon as these two get picked up, I'm going home."

Understanding dances in his eyes, and he steps forward to wrap me in a hug, a brief but comforting embrace. "Alright, take care of yourself, Tor. We'll catch up later. And please, *please* call me if you need anything. I know Ned was... well, Ned. But this is still a loss. Don't underestimate it, okay?"

"Okay. And thanks again." I smile at Ty warmly, letting him know his words and efforts are appreciated.

As he steps out the front door, I can't help but glance toward the mysterious man still seated outside. The moment Ty disappears, the stranger's gaze lifts, meeting mine through the glass. A jolt of something— apprehension mingled with an inexplicable attraction—tightens in my stomach. His eyes, dark and intense, seem to pierce through the distance, leaving me feeling exposed and oddly fascinated.

With a shake of my head, I turn away, leading the dogs to the door as their owners show up to pick them up. I then make sure the door is locked before flipping off the front lights. The comforting routine of closing up offers a semblance of normalcy, a distraction from the unsettling exchange and the draining day.

Retreating to my office, I aim to finish the day with one last task—an email to our clients, thanking them for their under-standing during the brief chaos of Ned's passing. He'd handled the behind-the-scenes business of the shop, so there was no need to break the news in a heavy sort of way. I get to work, the familiar click of keys under my fingers soothing, a mundane task that grounds me.

Mid-sentence, the sound of the back door opening breaks the silence. Assuming it's Ty, perhaps having forgotten something, I call out without looking up. "Forget your keys again?"

But the silence that follows isn't right. Ty would've responded with a joke or a quip, filling the room with his presence. A prickling sense of unease crawls up my spine, the earlier tension resurfacing as I realize the heavy silence might not be Ty's to break.

Stepping out of my office, the quiet of the shop presses in on me, unsettling in its emptiness. No sign of Ty or anyone else. Confused, I pivot back toward my office, the faint echo of my own footsteps a stark reminder of how alone I am.

Just as I sit down, I feel a presence behind me. I gasp when I find the man from the park bench and leap out of my chair.

He stands like a statue, filling the doorway with his imposing form. Up close, he's even more intimidating. He's tall, his frame blocking out the dim light from the hall, broad shoulders tapering down to a narrow waist. His dark hair is cut short, practical yet somehow managing to add to his rugged allure. The scars marking his face, evidence of a life I can barely imagine, don't detract from his looks; if anything, they lend him a sort of raw, undeniable edge. Dressed in a tailored suit that seems at odds with his bouncer-like build, he exudes an air of calm, professional composure almost more potent than if he'd carried a gun.

Despite my fear, my pussy clenches at the sight of him. No man has *ever* made me feel this way before. My heart races, fear mingling with a reluctant fascination as I instinctively reach for the scissors on my desk, gripping them tightly enough to feel the metal bite into my palm. He notices the movement but only smirks, as if my attempt to defend myself is more amusing than anything else.

"My condolences for your loss," he says, his voice smooth, betraying none of the tension zinging through the air between us. His tone is rich, deep, so resonant I can feel it in my bones.

"My loss? How do you know about that?" I ask, trying to keep my voice steady, the scissors gripped tightly in my hand.

He takes a step closer, and I fight the urge to step back. "I'm an acquaintance of Ned. And I'm here to let you know that he left behind a sizable debt with our organization and used this business as collateral." He gestures to the building that surrounds us. "I'm here to collect."

Our organization. Doesn't take a genius to know what that means.

The words hit me like a physical blow, my mind reeling at the implications. "You think I have his money?" Fear drips from my words, despite my attempts to project confidence. The scissors in my hand feel more useless by the second. Trying to use them as a weapon would end up with me disarmed and bent over the desk, his hand on the back of my neck.

His gaze is unwavering, analyzing my every reaction. " The debt needs to be settled."

The reality of my situation crashes down on me, the danger Ned has left in his wake now standing in my office, embodied by this calm, dangerously attractive man. My grip on the scissors tightens, not out of any real hope of defense, but because it's the only action I can take in a situation that feels increasingly beyond my control.

I'd known Ned was involved with the mob. Hell, as much as I hate to admit it, his mob ties were one of the things that attracted me to him. I'd always had a thing for bad boys, immature though such an inclination might be. But he was a low-level guy, not high up enough in the ranks to get himself wrapped up in any real, dangerous intrigue.

Or so I'd thought.

Shock paralyzes me for a moment. The idea that Ned, despite all his faults, would get us caught up in something like this, to put my business—my dream—in such danger, is almost too much to take.

"Sir, I have no idea what you're talking about."

There is something about him, something that urges me to speak to him with deference.

He nods, as if he's already factored my ignorance into his calculations. "Maksim Morozov," he says, correcting with a calm that belies the bombshell he's just dropped. "Call me Maksim. And you're Victoria Olsen. Though your friends call you Tory."

God, how much does he know about me?

I shake my head, desperation edging into my voice. "Listen, Maksim, I don't have any money to spare. This place isn't exactly a gold mine. We've only just started to see a profit."

His eyes flicker to the scissors I'm still clutching, a ghost of a smirk playing on his lips. "I'm not going to harm you. You can put those down while we chat."

I'm not convinced, my grip tightening rather than loosening. "I think I'll hold on to them, thanks. It's not every day a strange man corners me in my office demanding money I don't have."

Something shifts in Maksim's gaze then, a flicker of respect, maybe, for my refusal to be cowed. It's disarming, unsettling even, to see this hint of approval from a man who represents a world I want no part of.

"Ned died of a heart attack," I blurt out.

Maksim's expression is unreadable, his eyes holding mine in a steady gaze that gives nothing away. "I know. And I'm sorry for your loss, as I said. All the same, there's the reality of the debt. I'm here to collect, and that's what I intend to do."

I'm standing on a precipice, the ground crumbling beneath my feet, and Maksim Morozov, with his calm demeanor and dangerous allure, is the enigma at the heart of my turmoil.

CHAPTER 2

MAKSIM

"My relationship with Ned ended nearly a year ago," she declares, her eyes narrowed in sharp anger. "And he's been nothing but a headache since."

Her blunt honesty only deepens the intrigue, peeling back layers of respect and a curiosity I hadn't expected to feel.

"Quite a way to talk about an ex-lover," I say.

"Well, there's no reason to bullshit you."

"I can respect that."

I've crossed paths with countless faces, dealt with every type imaginable, but never have I been blindsided by attraction like this. This was supposed to be just another shakedown, nothing out of the ordinary for a man in my line of work.

Yet, here I am, standing in this cramped pet daycare office, completely thrown for a loop by this woman.

Her red hair, an untamed flame, and the resolve in her stance screams defiance. The scissors in her grip, her readiness to fight rather than cower, speaks volumes about her courage and tenacity. Traits that stir something within me, a heady mix of admiration and an arousal that's as unexpected as it is intense. Her face is gorgeous, stunning, with plump lips, blue eyes, and gorgeous features dusted with freckles.

Thinking about the debt her deadbeat boyfriend left behind, I can't wrap my head around how an idiot like Ned ended up with a woman of her caliber.

She's wearing a black dress -most likely funeral attire- that hugs her shapely figure. Her work apron is tied tightly, outlining the full breasts beneath. Even with her brandishing a weapon, all I can think about is hiking up that dress, peeling down her panties, and...

Focus, Maksim.

She's standing her ground, those fiery eyes locked on mine, scissors still in hand. "You need to leave," she states, voice steady, but I can tell there's a storm brewing behind those words.

I glance down at the scissors, a smirk playing on my lips as I entertain the thought of how far I'd need to push her before she'd actually go through with stabbing me, potentially ruining one of my favorite suits in the process. I let out a chuckle, genuinely impressed by her gumption.

Her response is immediate, her eyes narrowing into slits. "If you think I'm some helpless woman, you've got another think coming," she warns, her stance unwavering.

"I don't doubt for a second that you can take care of yourself," I tell her, my amusement fading into a blend of respect and curiosity. "Part of me wants to believe you about the money," I continue, weighing my words carefully. "'Then again," I ponder aloud, "a woman who's willing to fight for her life is also one willing to lie for it."

"Screw off," she fires back, not missing a beat, her resolve clear. "I'm no liar. You're getting me confused with my asshole ex."

My hand slips into my pocket, fingers brushing against the small listening device I always carry for shakedowns. It's there, reassuring in its presence, along with the one I'd already planted in her car earlier.

I'm quite certain I've got this woman pegged, but I need more information. I need her to keep talking.

Now, she's demanding space, a bold move. "Step out of my office," she orders, trying to reclaim some semblance of control over the situation. I can't help but smirk. Brave, indeed.

"Very well."

I concede, stepping back, allowing her the illusion of control, if only for a moment. She exits the office quickly, her movements brisk, trying to put as much physical distance between us as she can.

I take advantage of the moment, leaning down, feigning interest in her email, blatantly ignoring her as she snaps, "Hey! Get away from my desk."

As I'm leaning over her desk, pretending to give a damn about whatever's on her screen, I smoothly pull the listening device from my pocket. It finds its new home among the pens in one of her cups—perfect camouflage. It won't be spotted, and the acoustics of this makeshift hideout are ideal for picking up every word.

All the while, she's laying into me again, her voice spiked with that fiery command for me to exit her sacred space.

"Get the hell out of my office," she insists, barely containing her frustration. "I'm going to call the cops."

"Fine," I concede with a shrug, playing the part of the obedient visitor for now.

With another deft move as I rise, I withdraw a second camera from my other pocket, placing it on one of the office shelves, making sure it's pointed at the main space of her office.

As I turn to leave, something on the wall catches my eye—a Murphy bed, folded up against the wall. "You don't see those too often these days," I comment, my curiosity piqued.

She flicks her eyes over. "Came with the place." And not another word.

I step out of her office, but not without noticing the odd look she gives me at the mention of the bed. I can't help but grin, turning back to her with a parting shot. "I bet a small business owner like you has spent more than a few nights sleeping here."

It's a calculated guess, but her eye-flashing reaction confirms it. Then I notice the bags of personal items against the wall. Does she *live* here?

"You need to leave now, or I'll call the police," she threatens again, her voice laced with both bravado and desperation. Predictable and amusing all the same.

I can't help but chuckle at that, the sound rumbling deep from my chest. "You really think calling the cops is a threat to me?" I counter, shaking my head. "There's a greater than fifty-fifty chance that whatever cop shows up will be on my payroll."

Her frustration is palpable, but she's quick to retort, clinging to whatever leverage she thinks she has left. "There's no point in you being here anyway. I don't have the money. It'd be like squeezing blood from a stone."

I lean in, my voice dropping to a more serious tone. "Part of my job is finding out just how to extract cash—stone or not," I tell her, my gaze locking onto hers.

I throw another glance at the Murphy bed, and I catch something in Tory's eyes, a flicker that's hard to place. For a moment, it almost looks like lust. The sight sparks an impulse in me, raw and unfiltered.

Is she thinking the same thing I am, about the sorts of fun we could have on that bed? I make a decision.

"I can erase your debt," I suggest, the words slipping out with an ease that surprises even me, "if you want to come back in here and pull this Murphy bed down."

The suggestion hangs in the air between us, charged and dangerous. I watch, fascinated, as a storm of emotions battles across her face. Disbelief, anger, temptation—they all make their appearance, each vying for dominance.

In this moment, with the tension thick enough to cut, Tory stands before me, literally the most beautiful woman I've ever seen.

CHAPTER 3

TORY

His suggestion hits me like a slap in the face. I want to leap at him with the scissors still clutched in my hand, just for the insult of it, to cut that stupid grin right off his face for even thinking I'm that type of woman.

Fury boils over, and I let him have it.

"Who the hell do you think you are?" I spit out, the words sharp as knives. "You could be behind Ned's death, for all I know, and here you are, *propositioning* me? What an asshole! Asking for sexual favors to erase a debt? Hell fucking no!" I'm pacing back and forth now, every word fueled by shock, anger, and disbelief. I don't take my eyes off him. "That debt isn't even mine, so there's no way in hell I'm paying it in any form."

Maksim just watches me, that infuriatingly amused look plastered on his face as if this whole confrontation is a game to him. It's maddening, the way he manages to look both dangerous and undeniably sexy with just a smirk.

I throw another truth at him, hoping to wipe that smug look off his face. "Ned is dead. I have no clue what he did with the money he borrowed."

His response is cold, detached. "Ned's death is of no consequence to me." He pauses, his eyes locking onto mine. "He told me the money was for this business you two opened together. That's what matters. And that makes it your responsibility." He glances back at the kennel area.

The revelation of what Ned did feels like another blow that knocks the wind out of me. It's not just the audacity of his proposition now; it's the sinking realization of how deep Ned's lies have dragged me.

The gravity of the situation settles in, the danger, the betrayal, all of it weaving a noose around my neck. And Maksim seems to think it's all so goddamn funny.

I don't back down, my voice steady, laced with steel. "I never saw a dime of that money. That man? He expected me to pay him for the privilege of his help when we were together. This mess? It's not my problem."

Maksim moves closer, his presence towering, undeniably threatening. "It very much is your problem," he counters, his voice low, a dangerous edge to each word. "You own the business where the money was supposedly invested. You will pay the debt."

Time seems to slow between us, a silent standoff. I refuse to break eye contact, refuse to show any hint of weakness. And though his stance screams threat, there's an undercurrent of something else between us—lust. It's there, unmistakable in the way he looks at me, a raw desire that's as surprising as it is unsettling.

His gaze holds mine, intense, charged. The air between us crackles with an energy that's hard to define.

Despite the danger, despite the anger, I'm acutely aware of him—not just as a threat, but as a man. A man whose interest in me is more than just professional. The realization sends a thrill of power through me, even as it complicates everything further.

Finally, after what feels like an eternity, Maksim breaks our intense stare-off. But it's clear he's doing so on his terms, not because I've won any sort of victory. My heart hammers against my ribs as he reaches into his suit jacket. I'm half-expecting to see the glint of a gun. Instead, he pulls out a fancy pen, the kind that looks more at home in executive boardrooms than a pet daycare.

He leans over the counter, scribbling something on a notepad I've left out. "I'm writing down two numbers," he explains without looking up. "First, the amount you owe. Second, my business line." He pauses, finally meeting my gaze again. "Call me when you figure out how you're going to pay me."

Then, he steps closer, way too close. The heat from his body envelops me, and I'm suddenly aware of his scent, expensive cologne and something inherently masculine. He towers over me, his presence dominating the cramped space. It's intimidating, how small and vulnerable he makes me feel, a sensation that causes a confusing rush of fear and arousal to bolt through me.

"Expect another visit soon," he says, his voice low, sending shivers down my spine. He turns to leave.

Despite everything, despite my anger, my fear, and the indignation boiling inside me, I find my gaze trailing down, unable to resist stealing a glance at his retreating form, how gorgeous his ass looks in those perfectly tailored slacks.

As the door closes behind him, leaving me alone with my thoughts and the scribbled numbers on the notepad, I'm forced to confront the reality of my situation.

Frozen in the aftermath of his departure, it takes me several long seconds to snap out of my daze. Annoyed with myself, I rush to the back door through which he entered and exited, slamming the lock home. I chastise myself for the oversight of leaving it open, especially today. As if on cue, rain starts to fall, a soft patter that quickly grows into a downpour.

It takes every ounce of my will to finally move away from the door, my steps heavy as I approach the notepad he left on the counter. The number he wrote down, his handwriting impossibly neat, is stark against the white paper—a figure so high, it might as well be a sentence rather than a sum. Tears of frustration blur my vision, a mix of anger at Ned, at the situation he's left me in, and a bewildering attraction to a man who should repulse me on every level.

What am I going to do? The question echoes in my mind, a relentless tide of worry and despair. Ned's betrayal feels like a knife in the back, a wound made all the worse by the realization that even if he had lived, my store, my dream, was nothing more than collateral to him—a means to an end he had no hope of fulfilling.

Exhausted, emotionally spent, I drop into my chair at my desk, my gaze inadvertently catching the Murphy bed. A stark reminder of the many nights I've already sacrificed for this place. With a sigh, I bury my face in my hands, the weight of the world pressing down on me.

As the rain beats down outside, I ponder the impossible choices ahead, the paths I might have to walk, and the parts of myself I'm only now beginning to understand.

CHAPTER 4

MAKSIM

Dinner with the love of my life. What more could a father want?

As I sit across from Adelina, my four-year-old girl, her excitement fills the room. The soft glow of the dining room chandelier dances in her eyes as she chatters about her day, about the ballet recital she's been tirelessly preparing for. Her enthusiasm is infectious, even to a man like myself, accustomed to concealing his emotions behind a veil of calculation and control.

"Papa, Ms. Elena says I'm getting better. She says I might be ready for the solo part!" Adelina's voice is full of hope and pride, her small hands gesturing with every word she speaks.

I can't help but see her mother, Ana, in her in these moments—her grace, her passion for dance. It's both a comfort and a pang of loss. "That's wonderful, Ade. Your mother would have been so proud to see you dance," I say, my voice steady, despite the turmoil Ana's memory always stirs within me.

Adelina's smile falters for a moment, a shadow of sadness crossing her features. "Do you think Mama can see me from where she is?"

I pause, the weight of her question grounding me. "Yes, I believe she can. And I know she's very proud of you, just like I am."

She nods, accepting this, and quickly bounces back to her usual bubbly self. "I'm going to practice every day so I can be the best!"

"Being the best requires discipline and hard work. I have no doubt you'll achieve whatever you set your mind to," I encourage, my words deliberate, aimed to instill the values that have guided my own path—though I hope hers will be far less fraught with shadows.

Adelina giggles, clearly pleased with the conversation. "Will you come to see me dance?"

"Nothing could keep me away," I assure her.

My commitments to the family business are always secondary to the promises I make to her. It's a balance, a careful orchestration of priorities that few in my position might understand. But Adelina is my number one, a fact I've made abundantly clear to everyone, from my father to the men who operate under me.

As Adelina chatters on, her excitement about the ballet recital painting her features with a joy I rarely allow myself to feel, I can't help but draw parallels between her and her mother. "You're so much like your mother," I find myself saying.

"Why do you say that, Papa?" Adelina asks, curiosity lighting up her eyes. "Is it because we're both dancers?"

"It's not just the dancing," I explain, watching her closely. "You have her smile, Ade. The same one that could light up a room." As the comparison settles between us, her smile falters into a sigh.

"I wish I could remember her," she murmurs, a shadow of longing crossing her young face.

Irina, our matronly housekeeper and Adelina's de facto nanny, chooses that moment to step in. Her timing, as always, is impeccable. She catches the tail end of our conversation, and her expression shifts into one I've come to know all too well—the look that says she believes it's high time I find a wife, a mother figure for Adelina.

"Alright, Ade," she says, her Russian accent thick. "Time to get ready for bed. If you cooperate, we can have a little sherbet before I tuck you in."

"Yay!"

Irina takes Adelina upstairs and I'm left alone with my thoughts. The day is over for my little girl, but there's still business to attend to for myself. My father wishes to meet with me, to have one of his little meetings that I wonder, at times, are more about demanding my time than actual necessity.

I prepare myself an espresso, my mind already shifting gears to the tasks awaiting me. Irina comes down a bit later, likely off to the kitchen for Ade's dessert.

"I'll be home late," I inform her.

"You know, a beautiful wife would keep you home more," she retorts, a smile on her lips.

I laugh. "Irina, why don't you just marry me and solve all our problems?"

"Don't threaten me with a good time, as they say. Now, shoo. Don't keep that grump of a father of yours waiting." Adelina's voice calls out for her, pulling her attention away from our banter.

Once alone, I glance at my watch, the sleek hands indicating it's time to shift gears from family to business. I leave the warmth of home behind, stepping out into the crisp Chicago evening.

The drive to my father's place isn't long, but the few miles span a world apart. We both reside in an exclusive gated community in Lake Forest, a haven for Chicago's elite. His mansion dwarfs my own spacious, five-bedroom home, a silent testament to the hierarchy within our family, though I've never felt lacking—not in space or in stature.

As I navigate the familiar route, the grandiosity of my father's residence looms ahead, its opulence a sharp contrast to the simpler, albeit comfortable, life Adelina, Irina, and I lead. Aleksey, my ambitious half-brother, also calls this affluent neighborhood home, though our paths seldom cross outside the obligatory family gatherings.

The security detail outside of my father's estate recognizes my car immediately, waving me through with a nod of respect. Tiffany, my father's wife and Aleksey's mother, greets me at the door. Her appearance, ever the epitome of luxury and cosmetic perfection, prompts the customary exchange of pleasantries as I peck her Botoxed cheek—a gesture of politeness rather than affection.

"Igor is in his office," she informs me, her tone light yet carrying the undercurrent of the family dynamics that dictate our interactions.

"Thank you, Tiffany," I reply, my voice even.

The path to my father's office is as familiar as it is foreboding. Igor Morozov, patriarch, businessman, and sometimes adversary, waits with Aleksey by his side. The air in the room is charged, a mix of anticipation and underlying tension that's become a hallmark of our gatherings.

Aleksey, leaning against the polished mahogany desk, doesn't notice my entrance. His physical presence—taller than average, with a build that speaks to years of disciplined physical training, his dark hair slicked back in a manner that attempts to imitate our father's authoritative style—contrasts sharply with the petulance that often marks his countenance and demeanor. He's speaking animatedly, unaware of my observation.

"...and this pet daycare owner, she's yet to settle Ned's debt. Quite the peach, too," Aleksey remarks with a leer, unaware of the line he's treading. His voice carries a mix of amusement and disdain, a combination I've grown accustomed to navigating. "Gorgeous, in fact. Makes me wonder what she looks like underneath that dog-hair-covered apron she wears."

He laughs loudly at his own joke as Father rolls his eyes.

I remain silent, my entrance stealthy as a shadow, allowing him to continue unchecked. His comment about Tory irks me—unprofessional, unnecessary. Yet, I choose not to react. In this game, every emotion displayed is a weakness exploited.

Only when he pauses, perhaps sensing the shift in the room's atmosphere, do I make my presence fully known. "Father, Aleksey," I greet, my tone neutral, revealing nothing of my thoughts.

My brother turns, momentarily surprised, then quickly masks it with a broad grin, coming over and clapping me on the back as if we're allies rather than rivals held together by blood. "Maksim! Just the man I wanted to see," he declares, reaching for the scotch on the desk. "Drink?"

I nod, accepting the gesture for what it is—a play at camaraderie, as transparent as it is necessary.

"Thank you," I reply, taking the glass he offers.

Our father sits behind an imposing desk that's as much a barricade as it is a piece of furniture. His age is belied by the depth in his dark eyes, the same eyes I've inherited. Age has only slightly stooped his broad shoulders, and his hair, though silver, remains thick and meticulously groomed. He's a man whose commanded fear and respect in equal measure, and even now, in his later years, his presence demands attention.

"Maksim," he starts, his voice carrying the weight of decades of unchallenged power. "Have you handled the matter with the woman? The debt owed by that fool?"

I stand before him, my posture relaxed but alert. "Yes, Father. It's being addressed," I respond, my tone even, betraying none of the complexity of emotions Tory's situation has stirred within me.

"And?" he probes further, his gaze sharp. "Has she complied? Or do we need to encourage her cooperation?"

"The situation is under control," I assure him, aware of the unspoken implications of his 'encouragement.' "There's no need for further action at this point."

My father sits back, studying me with a scrutiny that's dissected and guided my actions since childhood. "Make sure it is, Maksim. We cannot allow debts to go unpaid. It sets a precedent."

"Understood," I reply.

The conversation shifts to other matters—territories, shipments, alliances—but my focus wavers. My thoughts drift to Tory, her defiance, her strength. And a realization that's as unexpected as it is unsettling: I'm considering forgiving her debt.

Not just forgiving it but erasing it entirely, an action that defies the very principles I've been raised on. And beyond that, the burgeoning desire to ask her out, to explore the connection that, despite all logic, seems to draw me to her.

The meeting with my father concludes with the usual assurances and directives, but as I take my leave, the weight of my thoughts anchors me. The decision I'm contemplating marks a potential shift in my world's axis.

CHAPTER 5

TORY

The shop is quiet, the kind of silence you need after a day of chaos and barking dogs.

I'm alone, cleaning up, the rhythmic swish of my broom practically meditative. The door chimes unexpectedly, slicing through the stillness like a knife. My heart skips a beat as I look up and find Maksim standing there, imposing and just as infuriatingly sexy as he was the other night.

He's dressed slightly more casually than the full suit I've seen him in, instead opting for gray slacks and a white dress shirt, the sleeves rolled up just enough to show off his sexy-as-hell forearms. He marches into my shop like he owns the place.

Hell, in a few days, he just might.

"Your debt," he begins, his voice low, "can be wiped away. All I ask is for you to give me what I want." His eyes lock onto mine, searching, as if he's trying to gauge my reaction.

A laugh, short and absent of humor, escapes me. "What if there's been a change to the deal?" I challenge. My heart's thudding in my chest.

He raises an eyebrow in surprise. "What sort of change?"

"It's no longer just about what *you* want. It's about what *I* want too."

There's nothing more to be said.

He moves closer, his hands finding my hips with a certainty that sends shivers down my spine. He pulls me into a deep kiss, a rush of desire and power swirling between us, the shop around us fading into nothingness.

He presses me against him, his hardness against my thigh.

But it's what I want. His lips part, his tongue finding mine. God, he tastes good. His tongue probes me, my pussy growing wetter by the second. There's no resistance from me, even though I should know better than to give myself to a man like him, a man so dangerous.

He reaches behind me, pulling off my apron and tossing it aside. My hands are busy on the pearl buttons of his dress shirt, opening them one by one, exposing his upper body. His chest is covered in strange tattoos that look almost religious.

I sweep my hands over his massive, sculpted chest, his lips curling into a sneer of pleasure, as if he knows exactly what kind of an effect he's having on me.

Before I can spend too much time ogling him, Maksim wraps his huge arm around my waist, pulling me close.

Those dark eyes, deep pools of desire, are locked onto mine. He reaches down to the hem of my dress, pulling it up and exposing the light blue thong I have on.

I feel exposed, my gaze flicking to the window to make sure no one's watching. The store's closed, but still...

Thunder rumbles in the distance, rain coming down hard, but my attention is on Maksim, that hungry, sensual expression he wears as his hand moves up, up, all the way to my pussy. He touches me through the fabric of my panties, teasing my clit.

"Does that feel good?" he growls.

"So... so good."

"You're mine now," he says, his tone brooking no dispute. "All *mine*."

The pleasure is so intense all I can do is nod. He takes his hand away and I want it back so goddamn badly.

"Go to the counter," he says. "Now."

I feel like I'm under a spell. I do as he asks without hesitation, my legs a bit wobbly from the excitement, my steps ungainly.

"Pull your dress up."

I obey. I can feel his gaze locked onto my ass, devouring me with his eyes.

"Pull down your panties."

I do it. The air is cool against my bare pussy.

He steps over, his dress shoes clicking against the floor. He puts one hand on my hip, the other undoing his zipper. I close my eyes, ready to feel him, ready for Maksim to plunge inside, and-

Thump.

The train hits a bump hard enough to yank me from my fantasy. The dream shatters, leaving me blinking against the harsh fluorescent light of the L train. It's morning, still dark out, the early hours casting a blue tint over Chicago as it starts to wake.

I sit up, realizing I'd dozed off on my way to work. It was a fantasy, nothing more, yet it feels like a betrayal of my own resolve. Why him, of all people? Maksim Morozov, a man who represented the kind of danger I'd vowed to stay away from.

The train jostles along the tracks, carrying me closer to another day at the shop, another day fighting to keep my head above water. The dream, unsettling as it is, underscores the loneliness that's been my constant companion since Ned's mess became mine. It's a reminder of my desires, buried down deep but still there.

The sickest part of it was that I wasn't even coming from my home, but from Ty's place where he'd let me crash for the night and take a shower. I'd lost my apartment during the breakup with Ned, and by that point the shop had been so all-consuming that I hadn't had the time or the money to get another place.

When I'd found out the shop had an old-school Murphy bed in the back, that sealed the deal. The shop also came equipped with a shower stall, so I was all set. But occasionally I liked to sleep in an apartment and bathe in a larger shower. Ty offered often, but I didn't want to be a burden.

As the train pulls into my stop, I shake off the remnants of the dream, getting psyched up for the day ahead. Stepping off, the cold morning air bites at my skin, a harsh jolt back to reality.

I'm at the shop by the ungodly hour of 4:45 AM, the quiet before the storm. The first arrivals, two golden retrievers named Jack and Sam, whose owners are nurses pulling twelve-hour shifts, expect nothing less than their preferred doggie beds side by side, complete with an assortment of toys I laid out the night before.

The shop, a haven for pups Monday through Friday -closed on the weekends, thank God- quickly becomes a bustling hub of activity, a total contrast to the silence of the early morning.

By eight, Paws and Play is full to the brim, barks and playful yelps filling the air. The morning has been smooth, all things considered, until an overactive chihuahua named Mabel decides she's the alpha, challenging a poodle/lab mix merely interested in a friendly sniff.

Carting the shivering, yet defiant, attacker to a quieter spot, I lecture her on the importance of manners, though I'm fully aware my words are lost in translation. As I'm talking to her, the back door opens, a sound that now triggers a mixture of excitement and dread. For a split second, my heart leaps at the possibility—could Maksim have decided to visit during work hours?

The thought sends a wave of conflicting emotions through me. It's ludicrous, given the circumstances, yet I can't help but feel a twinge of disappointment when it's not Maksim who walks in but Nicky, our new hire.

Nicky, oblivious to the mini drama unfolding in my head, trudges in with a huge bag of dog food slung over his shoulder, grumbling about the early hour and the weight of his load. My heart, still racing from the irrational hope of seeing Maksim, settles back into its usual rhythm, chiding myself for even entertaining the thought.

"Morning, Tory," Nicky mumbles, not a morning person, as he takes the dog food to the storage area.

"Morning, Nicky. Thanks for bringing that in," I respond, forcing a smile, my mind still reeling from the rollercoaster of emotions triggered by a simple sound. I watch as Nicky hauls the massive bag of dog food across the shop floor. "Make sure you get the dipper out *before* you dump it into the barrel," I call out to him, not wanting a repeat of last week's fiasco. I put a smile on my face as I make the request.

He turns, a matching grin spreading. "Won't make that mistake again. Learned my lesson the hard way," he chuckles.

Nicky's got the sort of easy attitude and good nature that a job like this requires. He'll be a great fit here, even if he isn't a morning person and assuming I can keep this place open. With Ty unable to work until noon, Nicky's presence in the mornings has been a godsend.

As the morning rush begins to settle and we catch our breath, Ty makes his grand entrance right around lunchtime, his arms heavy with bags that carry the unmistakable aroma of Chicago beef sandwiches.

"Lunch is served," he declares with a theatrical flourish of his arms, placing the bags on the counter with a sense of ceremony only Ty could manage.

I'm starving, but the unmistakable sound of a dog whining draws my attention to the back of the shop.

"Go ahead, guys, eat up," I tell them, tearing my eyes away from the bag of food.

The issue is obvious as soon as I step into the back. Howard, our resident Great Dane and usually a model of canine decorum, has decided that right after his outdoor break was the perfect time to create an indoor doggie doo-doo disaster.

"Howie, I swear." Howard's all contrition, sitting on his paws and regarding me with those big brown eyes of his. "You're lucky you're a charmer."

With a resigned sigh, I grab the cleaning supplies, leaving Ty and Nicky to their meals. The mess is sizable -and stinky- but it's all part of the job—a job I genuinely love, despite its less glamorous moments. As I work, the shop fills with the sounds of canine contentment: playful yips, happy barks, and the soft snores of napping pups. It's this stuff, this chaos, that reminds me why I'm here, why I've poured my heart and soul and savings into this place.

In spite of everything, a smile forms as I work. Life is hard as hell at the moment, but at least it's on my terms. Well, aside from the little matter of the debt Ned left me that I'll never be able to pay.

In the midst of scooping Howard's latest contribution to the shop vibe, a voice breaks through the monotony.

"You know, you look beautiful when you smile like that."

The deep timbre is unmistakable, instantly pulling me from my focus. I spin around, poop shovel in hand, to find Maksim leaning casually against the door frame to the back area, a smirk playing at the corners of his lips.

The shock of his presence sends a wave of heat across my cheeks, my earlier frustrations forgotten in the flush of embarrassment. I suddenly remember the fantasy, remember bending over in front of the counter, his eyes on me...

"Maksim," I manage, my voice steadier than I feel. The absurdity of the situation isn't lost on me—here I am, standing in the middle of my doggy daycare, armed with a shovel full of dog doo, face-to-face with the one man who's been occupying too much of my thoughts lately, my cheeks flushed red from the fantasy still lingering in my thoughts.

"What are you doing here? This is an employees'-only area, anyway." I realize how ridiculous the words are as soon as they come out of my mouth, telling a mobster he can't just stroll into the back area of a doggy day care.

His gaze drifts to the shovel, then the bag. "Are you going to throw that at me?" The amusement in his voice is clear, but there's an underlying challenge there, too. "Maybe fling your little biological weapon with that shovel?"

I can't suppress the snort that escapes me. "You know, I'd like to," I admit, the words out before I can think better of them. It's the truth, though. Part of me relishes the thought of wiping that smug look off his face, even as another, far less rational part of me is acutely aware of the tension that always seems to crackle between us. Howard sits calmly, watching us with his big brown eyes.

The standoff, if it can be called that, is broken by my decision to deposit the bag into the nearest waste bin, the lid banging shut as I close it.

Once the immediate crisis is handled, I face Maksim again, trying to ignore the quickening of my pulse. "Why are you back?"

My tone is light, but there's an undercurrent of curiosity, and yes, a hint of wariness. After all, our last encounter was anything but ordinary, and his presence here, now, suggests this visit won't be, either.

Maksim pushes off from the door frame, taking a step closer, his expression unreadable. "I had business nearby," he begins, the explanation sounding more like a pretext. "Thought I'd check in on how you're managing the debt."

He steps over to Howard, scratching the top of the dog's head. Howard's all about it, leaning into Maksim's touch.

The mention of the debt brings a sharp focus back to the conversation. My stance shifts, defensive yet defiant. "I'm managing," I assert, unwilling to show any sign of weakness. "But I doubt that's all you came here for."

He nods, giving Howard one more scratch before turning his attention to the rest of the shop. I glance through the windows that look out onto the front of the store. Ty and Nicky are watching with careful eyes. Ty holds up his phone, mouthing "call the police?" I shake my head.

"I wanted to see the business Ned used as collateral, while it's still open," Maksim says, his gaze sweeping across the shop with a curious intensity.

With a shake of the shovel, I gesture to the chaos around us. "Well, it's not all that glamorous, as you can see. But it's mine and I love it," I assert, pride swelling in my chest for the world I've built.

His smile then, unexpected and disarmingly handsome, sends my heart into a frenzy. It's unsettling how a simple expression can unravel me, can make me forget, if only for a moment, the complexities and shadows his presence in my life represents.

"It's good to take pride in your work, to be in pursuit of your own goals." He glances over his shoulder at the city outside. "So many people out there... they're going through the motions, not sure why they're doing what they do."

"Thanks for the inspirational words," I say, a tinge of sarcasm to my voice. "Is there anything else?"

Maksim's gaze snaps back from the window, locking onto mine with an intensity that feels like a physical touch. I'm being impatient, urging him to leave, but he doesn't seem at all affected, as if the world runs on his time.

"People like us," he pauses, a subtle emphasis on 'us', "we make our own fate."

His words hang heavy in the air "People like us, huh?" I reply. "And here I thought I was just a small business owner, not a mob enforcer."

He doesn't flinch at my words; if anything, his smile widens just a fraction, as if my snark is exactly what he expects, what he admires.

"Forget it," I go on, not sure I want to hear the end of that thought. "Was there anything else, or can I get back to work?" My tone is sharper than I intend, a defense mechanism against the turmoil stirring inside me.

"You and I both know there's something else. Let's talk."

CHAPTER 6

MAKSIM

"I already told you, I don't have the money."

I narrow my eyes, a slight tilt of my head as I consider her words. "You've got quite the tone for someone in your position," I say, my voice low, carrying a weight meant to remind her of the gravity of her situation.

"And you've got quite the tone for someone barging into *my* shop demanding I pay you a debt that isn't mine."

The air between us crackles with tension.

"How much do you have?" I probe further, stepping into the space she's filled with attitude.

Her resolve falters under the pressure of my inquiry, my directness. My nearness. To my surprise, a tinge of remorse washes over me, seeing the fight in her eyes dim. It's unexpected, this feeling, and unwelcome in my world where emotions can be liabilities.

THE ARRANGEMENT | 41

"I'm just about broke," she admits, her voice barely above a whisper, the fierceness from moments ago replaced by a vulnerable honesty.

It's rare for me to feel anything close to regret in my line of work, but watching her, a woman fighting tooth and nail for what she loves, stirs something unfamiliar within me.

"We need to find a solution," I say, the hardness in my tone softened, just a fraction, by the glimpse of her struggle. It's not in my nature to offer concessions, but something about Tory makes me reconsider the usual paths I'd take.

"I have nothing," she says again, each word heavy with defeat. " Every penny goes back into this shop. I don't even pay myself. Ty's the only full-time employee I can afford. I also have a part-timer."

I glance over my shoulder. The one named Ty is in sight, but the other employee isn't sitting with him.

This news catches me off guard. I've had eyes on her, surveillance that's told me a lot, but I hadn't bothered to check the footage from her office recently. The fact that she's sacrificed personal comfort for her business speaks volumes. It's a dedication I hadn't fully appreciated, a grit that commands respect even in my world.

"The only way I could get close to paying off the debt would be to sell the shop," she continues. "And I won't do that."

Her admission hangs in the air. It's a moment of raw honesty that strips away the adversarial dynamic between us.

I'm silent for a moment, processing her situation, the depth of her predicament. Selling the shop, her dream, isn't just a financial transaction; it's the surrender of her very essence, something she's unwilling to do. And unexpectedly, I find myself not wanting her to face that choice.

"There might be another way," I say, the words surprising even me. My life, my business, it's not known for leniency or second chances. Yet here I am, contemplating alternatives for a woman who's defied me at every turn.

She looks up, hope mingling with suspicion in her eyes. "Another way?" she echoes, searching my face for a sign of what I might be proposing.

"Yes," I confirm, stepping closer, the space between us charged with a new, unexplored tension. "We can figure out a solution. One that doesn't involve selling your shop."

Her eyes narrow. "Oh. Your *other* offer. I almost forgot."

I open my mouth to speak, but before I can get even a word out, an employee—broad-shouldered, with an easy smile— interrupts my train of thought.

"Hey, are you a new client?" he asks, extending a hand. "I'm Ty, Tory's best friend and right-hand man around here."

For a split second, I'm on edge, but his demeanor is far from confrontational. Instead, he dives headfirst into what can only be described as an enthusiastic sales pitch.

"You've come to the right place if you're looking for a place for your pet. She's the heart and soul of this place. Hard-working, passionate... she's incredible."

I raise an eyebrow, amused by the misunderstanding. "Is that so?"

Ty nods, leaning in as if sharing a well-known secret. "Absolutely. You won't find a better place in the city."

It's almost comical, how off the mark he is, believing my presence here to be of a personal nature. Yet, I play along, curious to see where this leads. "Really? She sounds remarkable."

"Yeah, and she's got a way with the dogs, and people, too. You're not gonna find anyone else like her," Ty continues.

Our conversation is suddenly cut off by a sharp yelp from the main area, pulling Ty's attention away. The yelp turns out to be from a chihuahua, its tiny frame shaking as it tries to escape the solitary area, somehow trapping itself in the process. Without thinking, I move toward the frightened animal, driven by instinct.

"Wait!" Tory's voice slices through the chaos, sharp with concern. "That's Mabel. She bites."

Her warning barely registers, the dog's distressed cries pulling at me. As I reach the trembling chihuahua, I drop to my knees, speaking in soft, soothing Russian, words from a childhood I keep locked away.

"It's okay, little one," I say quietly, gently freeing her from her predicament. To my surprise, she doesn't snap or struggle; instead, she curls into me, seeking comfort.

Turning back to Tory, I find her staring at me, a look of sheer amazement on her face. It's a moment, suspended in time, where the usual barriers between us seem to crumble.

"Was that Russian?" she asks. I can't help but smirk, the dog still nestled against me, its earlier panic forgotten.

"Animals understand kindness, no matter the language."

Tory steps closer, her gaze lingering on the scene before her. "I've never seen her calm down so quickly with anyone else. That was impressive."

The compliment, simple as it is, sparks an unfamiliar warmth.

"She was scared, that's all. Anyone would've done the same," I say, attempting to brush off the significance of the moment.

But Tory shakes her head, her eyes still fixed on mine. "Not like that. You have a way with her. Thank you."

CHAPTER 7

TORY

The sight in front of me defies belief. Mabel, normally a trembling ball of nerves around anyone but women, is pressed against Maksim as if he's the safest place in the world. Watching the little dog find solace in the arms of a man she's just met—especially a man like Maksim—my heart softens a bit more toward him.

Ty speaks up, "Man, you must have some kind of magic touch with animals."

Maksim offers a shrug. "I have a daughter," he says simply. "She taught me gentleness."

The admission strikes me, painting a picture so at odds with the man I thought I knew. The idea of him as a doting father nearly floors me. There's a depth to him, a complexity that's both intriguing and alarming.

Ty, never one to miss a beat, turns the conversation, his tone playful but pointed. "So, you're married?" he asks, testing the waters in a way that's bold, a little reckless, and painfully obvious.

Maksim's response is immediate, his gaze finding mine. "I am not," he confirms. "I was actually hoping Tory would do me the honor of going to dinner with me."

The room seems to pause, the air charged with anticipation. Ty, sensing the shift, lets out a sigh and takes the chihuahua from Maksim. The dog, not pleased with the change in custody, growls her displeasure. "Easy, girl," Ty soothes as he turns to me. "Don't let your food get cold, Tory."

He carries the chihuahua out of the room, leaving me to process Maksim's unexpected invitation. The contrast of this moment with the earlier tension is disorienting. Maksim Morozov is asking me out to dinner. Not as a demand, but as... what? An offer? A date?

My mind races, torn between the practicality that's guided my life these past months and the flicker of attraction I can't seem to quell. Maksim is dangerous, a fact I haven't forgotten. But he's also a father, evidently, and a man capable of gentleness and warmth. The contradiction draws me in, despite my reservations.

The moment hangs between us, charged and heavy. I want to say yes, to accept the dinner invitation that feels like an olive branch and a chain all at once. But the memory of his initial 'deal' crashes over me like a cold wave—the offer that had nothing to do with dinner and everything to do with a transaction I can't stomach. He had dangled freedom from my debt in exchange for a night in his bed, a proposition that had soured my view of him from the start.

Drawing in a deep breath, I find the courage to hold my ground, to confront the man and the people behind him with the full force of my integrity. "I don't care what you or your people do to me," I begin, my voice steady despite the tremor of fear that threatens to undermine my resolve. " And I don't know what you have in mind with this *date*, but I won't have sex with you to clear they debt."

His reaction is not what I expect. A chuckle, low and surprisingly warm, escapes him as he shakes his head, a gesture that seems almost... amused.

"The debt is already cleared," he says simply with a sweep of his hand, as if it's the most natural conclusion in the world.

"Wait, what?" I manage to stammer out, my voice betraying the turmoil of emotions churning inside me. "A few minutes ago, you were telling me I still had to pay. Asking me how much money I had."

His response is almost nonchalant, a slight tilt of his head as he considers his words. "Consider it my good deed for the year," he says, but there's a depth in his gaze that suggests it's more than just a whimsical act of charity. " I don't want any obligations between us. I'd like to take you out on a date. But only if you say yes because you want to, not because you feel you have to."

His admission sends my mind into a tailspin. There are a million reasons to reject his offer: the shadow of the dirty business clinging to him like a second skin, the veiled threats looming over my shop, the unsettling possibility that he or someone he commands could be behind Ned's untimely demise.

He's woven from danger, a fabric too volatile, too uncertain for someone like me, who craves stability, who's fought tooth and nail for a semblance of peace in a world that seems constantly against her. He's unpredictable—this thought echoes in my head, a mantra that should dictate my next words, guide me toward the safe choice, the smart choice.

Yet, as I look into his eyes, seeing the sincerity I hadn't expected from a man of his reputation, my resolve wavers. There's an honesty there, a genuine interest that goes beyond the transactions and power plays that define his world. It's disarming, unsettling in its intensity.

Before I can marshal my thoughts, before I can weigh the consequences one last time, my mouth betrays me. "Yes," I hear myself say, the word slipping out in a rush of adrenaline.

His smile, warm and unexpected, slices through the tension. "May I have your number?" he asks, a simple request loaded with implications.

I find myself moving toward the counter, almost on autopilot, and grab one of the business cards in my apron pocket. As I scribble down the digits, the reality of what I'm doing sets in. I'm giving Maksim Morozov, a man who both intimidates and intrigues me, a direct line into my life.

He takes the card from me, our fingers brushing in the exchange. The brief contact sends a shiver up my arm, an electric charge that's both startling and exhilarating.

Without warning, he lifts my hand to his lips, kissing the back of my knuckles. The gesture, so unexpectedly gentle from a man of his status, ignites a response in me that's both immediate and intense. I'm reeling from the rush of sensation, the physical reaction undeniable and disconcerting.

"I'll text you. I'm thinking this Friday," he says, grounding me back to the moment.

All I can manage is a nod, my mind still racing from the contact, from the anticipation of what's to come. As he turns to leave, Ty and I stand there, a silent duo watching him exit the shop. There's a palpable shift in the air, a sense that something significant has just been set into motion.

CHAPTER 8

There I stand, in the middle of the chaos that is my life, feeling a whirlwind of emotions as the door swings shut behind Maksim. The air feels different, charged with something I can't quite name, leaving me more stunned than I'd like to admit. It's as if his presence has shifted something fundamental in the room, in me.

Howard, the Great Dane, ambles over to me, his big brown eyes seemingly filled with an understanding that goes beyond his canine senses. He whines softly, looking toward the door Maksim just exited through, and I wonder if he's expressing a sentiment I'm not ready to acknowledge myself: a part of me is sad to see him go.

Before I can dive too deep into that unsettling realization, Nicky's hand, waving frantically in front of my face, snaps me back to reality. "Hey, Tory."

"What's up?" I manage, trying to shake off the lingering thoughts of Maksim.

"I need to head out a bit early today," Nicky starts, his voice laced with a strange intensity that immediately catches my attention. "Just got a call from my girlfriend. Her car broke down. That okay? I can stay later tomorrow and do your closing duties."

There's something in his tone, a seriousness that's not typical of the laid-back Nicky I've come to know. It's enough to make me take a closer look, to really see the worry etched into his features.

"Sure," I respond, more out of concern for his uncharacteristic behavior than anything else. "Hope everything's okay."

He offers a quick, grateful smile, hastily gathering his belongings. "Thanks, boss. Really appreciate it," he says before rushing toward the door, his usual easygoing demeanor replaced by urgency.

As the door closes behind him, I find myself once again caught in a moment of reflection. The shop, usually my sanctuary from the unpredictability of life, suddenly feels too quiet, too still.

By 6:30, the last dog has trotted out the door with her owner, leaving the shop in a rare state of quiet. Ty and I retreat to my small office, a space crammed with paperwork and dreams, to tackle the never-ending battle with the books. The numbers sprawl across the table between us. For the first time, we're teetering on the edge of profit, a milestone that seems both monumental and terrifyingly fragile.

"You need to start paying yourself, Tory," Ty insists, his tone serious. He's been on me about this for weeks, concerned that my all-in approach to the business is taking its toll. "Living out of this office is not good for you."

I sigh, rubbing the bridge of my nose as I lean back in my chair. "Just a few more months," I reassure him, more hopeful than certain. "Once we're on solid ground, I'll figure out a better setup."

Ty shakes his head, unconvinced. "And until then? I mean, seriously, you can shower and crash at my place whenever you want – God knows it's empty enough there now that Thomas and I are done and he's gone. But this..." He gestures vaguely at the cramped space that serves as my living quarters as much as my command center, "sorry, but you deserve better."

I can't help but laugh, a brief respite from the weight of our conversation. "What, you don't think the industrial dog shower is good enough?" I joke, trying to lighten the mood. "I'll be fine until we're on good footing. Really, Ty, I've got this."

He looks at me, a mix of frustration and concern in his eyes, but he knows better than to push the issue further. We've danced this dance too many times, and he understands my stubbornness as much as he worries about it.

Ty pivots to the date, already planning it out for me. Just tossing in the fact I'm stepping out with Maksim sends my nerves into overdrive. I mean, it's been a hot minute since I've been on any kind of date, let alone with someone like him.

"You're gonna nail it," Ty assures me with a chuckle, clearly finding my dating rust amusing. "Guys are all the same."

I roll my eyes. "Except Maksim isn't just any guy."

He throws me one of those over-the-top winks, adding, "Maybe so, but hey, just have fun. Maybe even... you know," he teases, miming a kiss and wiggling his eyebrows.

I launch a paperclip his way, a pitiful but immediate comeback. He catches it, laughing.

"You sure you don't want to stay over tonight? We can watch *Love Island*..."

"It's tempting. But I don't want to wear out my welcome."

"You're not even close to that, but I know better than to press. See you in the morning, Tor." With that, he's off, locking the door behind him.

So here I am, closing up shop alone with my racing thoughts and a simmering combination of excitement and outright terror. Going on a date with Maksim Morozov is no small deal. It's a leap into the unknown, a dive into deep waters where the current could either sweep me off my feet or pull me under. And despite the whirlwind of what-ifs, I'm somehow stepping right into it—no looking back.

Even though it's still early, I'm totally beat. I turn off the computer, grab my bag, and head to the bathroom to get ready for bed. I quickly change, taking off my stinky work clothes and putting on a long Taste of Chicago sleeping shirt.

Once I'm cozied up in the Murphy bed, my little makeshift slice of heaven in the shop, I give my phone a quick scroll. My heart's not in it, and before I know it, I'm chucking the phone aside. Maksim's taken up residence in my head, and man, he's not making it easy to think about anything else.

I'm turned on beyond belief and suddenly not so tired. Knowing what will cure my ills, I reach into the bag beside my bed and pull out my battery-operated boyfriend. After peeling off my panties, I flick on the vibrator and press it to my clit, just where I need it. The pleasure is immediately intense, and after taking a moment to get used to the warmth flowing through me, I close my eyes and drift away.

He waltzes into my office like a scene straight out of my wildest daydreams. The dim light from outside throws his shadow across the room, making him look both mysterious and ridiculously attractive.

"Maksim?" I blurt out. Even in my fantasies, I'm not sure how to handle him.

He doesn't waste time with small talk. A few steps and he's right there, pulling me close. His hands land on my hips, sending that familiar jolt of excitement through me. He squeezes my flesh, as if savoring the sensation of my curves underneath his touch.

"Tory," he says, and damn, if his voice isn't the sexiest thing.

My heart's thumping in my chest, but I manage to nod to him, and with my surrender, we're kissing. It's not just any kiss, though. It's like he's answering all the questions I didn't even know I had, and God, does it feel right. In that moment, with Maksim's lips on mine, the world outside might as well not exist. It's just him and me and this crazy-intense thing sparking between us. It's wild, reckless, and absolutely thrilling.

Back in the real world, I angle the vibrator so it hits my clit in just the right way.

In the fantasy we're stripping one another out of our clothes, Maksim undoing the clasp of my bra and sliding the straps down my shoulders. Every new bit of bare skin he covers in kisses, and my breasts are no exception. He licks and sucks my nipples, the pleasure intense.

I reach down and grab his cock through his slacks. He's rock-hard, practically throbbing in my grasp. He growls as I stroke him. Not able to wait a moment longer, I undo his leather belt and zipper, pulling down his pants and his boxer-briefs, his dripping manhood leaping out into my grasp.

"You taste so goddamn good," he says, his voice a sensual purr, totally irresistible.

Once more, his hands are on my hips. This time, he guides me back to the little Murphy bed and tosses me onto it, a squeal of delight shooting from my lips as I land, the springs squeaking underneath me.

He's standing before me like a damn Greek god, his power-ful, sculpted, tattooed body on full display, his hands on his hips, his cock spear-straight just above his slightly-pulled-down pants. He reaches down and grabs his shaft.

"You want this?" he asks.

"Are you kidding?"

He grins. "Then ask me nicely. Very, very nicely."

"Please?" I don't know what else to say.

He snorts and grins, as if more amused than anything else. "You're going to have to do better than that."

My eyes flick down to his cock, the pleasure of the vibrator back in the real world driving me crazy. "Pretty please?"

Another snort of amusement. He steps forward, his thickness bouncing with each stride. When he's close, looming over me, his cock only inches from my face, he leans down and takes my face into his hand from underneath.

"Better than that."

I lick my lips, the effect his command is having on me surprising me. And I love it.

"Please give me your cock."

"Please give me your cock *what*?"

It hits me what he wants.

"Sir."

"Good girl."

He pounces to me. His hands go to my wrists, pinning me down. Maksim is massive on top of me, his muscular body huge, blocking out everything else. I want him so badly I can't even stand it. I wrap my legs around him, pulling him close, guiding him inside.

He enters me with total ease, thrusting into me over and over again.

Back in the real world I'm thrashing around, moaning his name, holding the vibrator in place, imagining him driving into me again and again and again until...

"Mak-*siiiim*!" I almost scream his name.

The orgasm rips through my body, heat spreading outward and making me feel like I've lit up. I hold the toy in place, coaxing every last drop of delight out of the fantasy.

When I'm done, I flick off the vibrator and let it drop onto the bed, my arms and legs plopping onto the mattress. I'm totally spent.

The fantasy's over, and reality's returned. I can't help but wonder if I've seriously overplayed my hand this time. Going to dinner with a guy like him—have I just opened Pandora's box?

CHAPTER 9

MAKSIM

I n my study, scotch in hand, I watch the fire. Tonight, Adelina's at her grandparents', giving me a rare moment alone.

Tiffany, my stepmother, is a complex figure. She's great with Adelina, and for that, I'm thankful. But between us, there's always been tension. She sees me as a threat to Aleksey, her own son. It's clear I'm not her favorite person, but as long as she's good to my daughter, I can live with that.

The flames flicker, pulling my thoughts to Tory. Clearing her debt was a move against my usual play, driven by something I can't quite nail down. My father won't be happy to hear what I've done. It's a risk, stepping out of the shadows for something personal.

I've always played it safe, sticking to the shadows where I thrive. But with Tory, it's different. There's a pull there, something that's got me stepping into uncharted territory.

In this life, you don't get many chances at something genuine. I'm willing to take this one, see where it leads.

I settle behind the study desk and boot up my laptop. There's this twist in my gut, a hint of being a stalker, as I pull up the app connected to the camera in Tory's office. With her debt wiped clean, I've got no business keeping tabs on her like this. The right move is to disconnect the camera, cut the tie.

But I can't bring myself to do it.

I catch a bit of conversation between her and Ty, who's speaking in animated tones and waving his hands around. The sound's off, so I can't hear what they're saying – it's likely not important. Tory steps out, leaving the office empty for a spell before she comes back. I adjust the volume, turning it up.

There's a stretch of silence, just the mundane sounds of the shop, until I hear her laugh. It's a sound I haven't heard enough, light and genuine, cutting through the silence like a beam of light. It's beautiful, her laughter, drawing me in, holding me without effort.

I know I should shut it down, cut off this one-sided window into her world. But her laugh makes it impossible. It's a reminder of what's pulling me toward her, beyond debts or obligations. It's real, it's human, and it's utterly captivating.

Sitting there, lost in the sound of her laughter, I'm struck by the absurdity and the gravity of my situation. A man like me, finding something close to peace in the simple sound of a woman's laughter through a hidden camera. It's a contradiction that would be laughable if it weren't so damn compelling.

So I watch, and I listen, caught between the role I play and the man I might be, if things were different.

Ty and Tory exchange a few more words at her desk before Ty bids her farewell for the night. She springs out of her seat, grabbing a bag and heading into the employee bathroom, disappearing from sight.

This is where I should turn off the recording. What else could I possibly expect to see?

But I keep watching, hitting the fast-forward button until she's back in the frame. She's wearing nothing but a long tee shirt and panties, her shapely legs on display. My cock is pulsing to life, growing harder by the second.

She climbs into bed and looks at her phone for a few minutes before tossing it aside and reaching into the bag next to her bed. She pulls out something long and purple and I can't believe my eyes. A grin spreads across my face as I realize she's about to pleasure herself. I watch as she slips out of her panties and places the vibrator against her clit.

It's all I can take. Matching her urgency, I undo the buckle of my belt and pull my pants down enough for my cock to jump out. My eyes locked onto the screen, I take hold of my length and begin stroking, the pleasure instantaneous.

I turn up the volume on my computer, her soft moans pouring from the speakers. I don't know what she's using for inspiration, but whatever it is, she's soon thrashing back and forth, moaning and writhing.

"Maksim..."

I pause, my cock still in my hand.

Did I hear that correctly?

I rewind the recording, playing it again. Sure enough, it's my name she's moaning as she brings herself to orgasm. I grin, knowing she's as much on my mind as I am on hers.

In tandem, we pleasure ourselves. Soon her back is arching, my name coming from her mouth over and over as I bring myself to climax. With a hard grunt, I release at the same time she does. My eyes stay locked onto her body, my ears focused on her moans.

When I'm done, I clean myself off and close the laptop.

It should be enough. I've just come, which should quell my desire for the night.

But it doesn't. I still want her, and only one thing will satisfy my yearnings.

After composing myself, I hurry downstairs, my footsteps echoing through the expanse of my home. I grab my keys, throw on my coat, and head out into the night.

Before the sun rises, Tory will be mine.

CHAPTER 10

TORY

Sleep is a no-go tonight. Every time I shut my eyes, there's Maksim, front and center in my mind, stirring up a whirlwind of feelings I'm still trying to wrap my head around. It's like my brain's only got one track, and it's all him, all the time.

The more I try to calm down, the more worked up I get, tossing and turning in the bed that's starting to feel way too big and empty.

As I try to find a comfortable position, my phone lights up, cutting through the frustrating cycle of thoughts with a message that makes my heart skip a beat. The text is from Maksim, short and to the point:

Let me in.

Frowning, I'm off the bed in a flash, curiosity mixed with a whole cocktail of emotions as I make my way to the front door. Through the glass, I see him, and it's like my entire body goes on high alert, reacting to his presence in a way that's both exhilarating and a little terrifying.

Standing just on the other side of the glass, he's this imposing figure that somehow, in the quiet of the night, feels like he belongs here. My pulse races, and I'm acutely aware of every little detail—the way the streetlight casts shadows across his face, the expectant look in his eyes, the way my own body seems to lean toward him, as if drawn by some invisible force.

The moment feels loaded with possibilities, and I'm suddenly hyper-aware of the decision I'm about to make. Opening that door isn't just about letting him into the shop; it's about letting him into my world, crossing a line that's going to change things between us, one way or another.

My hand hesitates on the lock, my mind racing.

Screw it.

As I unlock the door and let him step inside, the air between us crackles. Quickly, I lock the door again, turning to face him, ready to demand an explanation.

"What are you doing here?" The words barely leave my lips before he's on me, his hands gripping me with a sureness that silences any further questions.

He doesn't answer with words. Instead, his lips crash against mine, a kiss so intense my thoughts scatter. My body reacts on instinct, pressing into him, drawn to the danger and allure he embodies.

"You want this, don't you?" His voice is a low murmur against my lips, as if he's reading my mind.

I can't manage words, just a nod, my body betraying my inner turmoil by responding to his every touch. Without another word, he lifts me effortlessly, carrying me toward the office. He sets me down gently on the Murphy bed, the makeshift nature of my living quarters seemingly forgotten in the moment.

"Tory," he breathes out, a question and a declaration all in one.

"Yes," I whisper, giving in to the torrent of emotions he's unleashed within me. It's a surrender, an acceptance of whatever this is between us, despite the million reasons I should hold back.

In the silence of the shop, everything else fades into the background. It's just Maksim and me, teetering on the edge of something neither of us fully understands but are too caught up in to question.

We kiss again, long and deep and sensual. The fantasy I had about him was only a few hours old, but already it was blown out of my mind by the reality of what was happening between us.

He takes the hem of my sleeping shirt and tugs it a bit. "I like your ensemble."

I laugh. "It's the kind of outfit you can expect when you come over unannounced in the middle of the night."

"As charming as it is, let's get it off." He pulls the shirt off, the air of the office cool against my skin.

Once the shirt's gone, I work on his buttons, unbuttoning them one by one. With a quick push, I throw off his shirt. Just like in my fantasies, he's sculpted and shredded and muscular, not a drop of fat on his body. And there are tattoos, just like I'd imagined, ink on his chest and shoulders and arms.

I don't have much time to stare. He hooks his thumbs under the waistband of my panties and pulls them down. They drop to my ankles and he quickly places his big, rough hand between my thighs. I moan at his touch, bucking into it, yearning for more.

More is just what he gives me. His hand finds my lips and I'm already soaking wet for him. Maksim's other hand effortlessly unclasps the back of my bra and I help him, slipping the straps over my shoulders. I'm bare before him, exposed in front of a man I've known for barely two days.

But it feels so goddamn right.

We kiss and he touches me, pleasure coursing through my body as he spreads me open and teases my clit. The intensity is so much I can't help but lean forward and rest my head against his big, round shoulder. Maksim places his other hand on the small of my back, keeping me against him.

"Keep touching me like that. Please. Please." The words come out on hot breath, and he seems to have no intention of stopping.

Each touch, each slow circle around my clit with his fingertip brings me closer and closer and closer until... I shut my eyes, letting out a silent shriek against his skin. Maksim brings me to a roaring orgasm, my legs shaking underneath me as I come. He holds me and touches me, making sure he can feel me as I come.

When the pleasure's faded, he guides me directly to the bed. Standing before me, he takes down his pants and underwear, his cock just inches away from my face. He's as long and thick as I'd fantasized, and all I can do at first is stare.

"Take me in your mouth."

It's one more commonality to the fantasy – Maksim telling me what to do. I want to object. But more than that, I want to obey.

So, I do. I lean forward, grasping his cock and placing my lips on his end. He growls with pleasure as I go to it, covering his head in kisses and licks. He reaches forward, slipping his hand into my hair and palming the back of my hand. He pushes gently but insistently, guiding me down his length.

Inch after inch, I take him into my mouth. Having him in my mouth, knowing I'm bringing him closer to orgasm with just my hand and lips and tongue turns me on like crazy.

His hand guides me, urging me to move faster and faster. I'm lost in the rhythm, feeling him shake a bit as he draws closer to release. All I can think about is him erupting in my mouth, covering my tongue in his seed.

"On your back."

Maksim doesn't give me the chance to finish him. He slides his dick out of my mouth and points to the bed. I do as he asks, laying back, my legs spread, my pussy clenched and wet. I can hardly take it.

He climbs on top of me, sitting back on his legs and grabbing my ankles, pulling me toward him. His hands clap down on my exposed ass, my eyes widening with the shock of impact. It feels *good*, weirdly good.

I reach down and grab his base, guiding him inside. He pushes his hips, entering me, penetrating me, my walls gripping him tightly as he stretches me out. He spreads my legs farther, my breasts bouncing as he drives inside.

"Tell me how my cock feels inside you," he says, leaning down and gazing at me with those dark, dark eyes.

"So good. So goddamn good." He grins slightly, and I know I've given him the right answer.

"Now, I want you to come for me. I want you to come on my cock. Is that understood?"

I've never been with a man like this before, one so confidently telling me what to do. It's unlike anything I've known before, and as much as part of me wants to bristle, another part of me wants to give in, to let him take the lead.

So I do. I release, focusing on the sensation of his big cock pushing into me, spreading me open, splitting me in two. I arch my back, the orgasm erupting and flowing through me.

Maksim joins me. He wraps his arm around me underneath my arched back and pulls me against him. He grunts hard, just like in my fantasy, as he spills himself inside me. I can feel his cock pulse as he comes, the rest of the world totally obliterated as we rise and fall together.

My chest expands and contracts, and he wastes no time pulling me against his powerful body. It feels *right* to be against him like this, to curl into his form.

Even in the immediate afterglow, there's no doubt in my mind that Maksim has unleashed an appetite in me only he can satisfy. And I look forward to feasting again and again.

CHAPTER 11

MAKSIM

The Murphy bed's not exactly spacious, but it's enough for this moment, her nestled against me as she drifts off. There's a clarity in the quiet, a certainty that she's what I've been looking for—not just for me, but for Adelina too, who's needed a mother figure for a long while now.

It's insane how quickly I feel this way toward her. I've only known Tory for a couple of days and I'm already considering her as a stepmother for my daughter? I should be chastising myself for such thoughts.

But they seem so right.

I'd stay if I could, wrap the night around us and forget the world outside. But I've got promises to keep, especially to Adelina. Breakfast plans with her aren't something I'm willing to break. She counts on me, and I won't let her down.

Leaning close, I breathe in the scent of Tory's hair, a moment of peace amidst the chaos of my life. She's sound asleep, worn out, and I know she's got her own early start tomorrow. With a silent reluctance, I carefully disentangle myself and get dressed, the quiet of the room heavy with the echoes of what's passed between us.

Before I go, I scribble a note, something to remind her of the connection we've shared tonight and the promise of what's to come.

Looking forward to Friday. Sleep well, Tory, I write, hoping the words convey more than just the sentiment, but the anticipation, the promise of more.

Leaving her in the dim light of her office-turned-bedroom feels like stepping away from a moment suspended in time. But the note, that small token, is a bridge to the next time we meet.

Silently, I make my exit, the weight of the night and the promise of the future mingling in my thoughts as I step out into the early morning. The city's quiet, the world unaware of the shift that's just occurred in my heart.

The morning drive takes me straight to the doorstep of my father's imposing estate, its vastness a testament to the Morozov legacy. The structure looms large, all sleek lines and expansive windows, a fortress masquerading as a home.

As I pull into the circular drive, Aleksey's car is impossible to miss. It's the kind of vehicle that doesn't just whisper wealth—it shouts it, chrome glinting in the morning light, as subtle as a gunshot. It irks me, his penchant for the ostentatious. In our line of work, discretion is key, but Aleksey's choices are a constant signal of excess.

I park my own car, its understated elegance a deliberate choice, and make my way to the front door. The cool metal of the handle gives way to the familiar warmth of the interior as I step inside. It takes but a moment before the quiet is shattered by the sound of tiny feet on marble.

Adelina, my heart, rushes into the entry hall with the unbridled joy only a child can muster. Her arms are thrown wide and I scoop her up without hesitation.

"Papa!"

"Princess!"

Her laughter fills the space, echoing off the high ceilings as her cheek presses against mine. She's still clad in her pajamas, a whimsical pattern of cartoons dancing across the fabric.

"I didn't know you were coming so early," she says into my shoulder, her words muffled but filled with sleep-tinged surprise.

Smiling, I kiss her cheek, setting her down with a gentle reminder. "Can't keep a beautiful girl waiting," I say, a hint of playfulness in my tone. "Now, go grab your things. I need to meet with *dedushka*."

"Okay, Papa. Can we get waffles?"

"We can get whatever you want."

She giggles, a sound that cuts through the heaviness of my world and darts off to get ready. I watch her go, her energy wild.

Tiffany steps into the hall, the picture of polished grace despite the early hour. "She was a pleasure, as always."

"Good to hear. And thanks again."

She smiles. "Happy to do it. Can I get you some coffee, Max?"

"No, thank you," I decline, keeping it brief. We're about to dive deeper into a morning catch-up when my father's voice cuts through any attempt at small talk.

"*Mak-siiim!*" His command booms from upstairs, unmistakable and urgent.

Tiffany's eye roll is quick, a shared moment of understanding between us. "As you can hear, he's already deep into work," she quips, a hint of dry humor lacing her words. "I'll help Adelina get dressed."

I nod, acknowledging the situation with a resigned sigh, and make my way upstairs. The familiarity of the estate guides me to his office, a room that's as vast and imposing as the man himself.

Aleksey is in the office, his presence noted with a mere nod —a silent acknowledgment of the complexities that bind and divide us. My focus shifts to my father, Igor, a figure of authority ensconced behind his desk. His question pierces the morning calm, direct and loaded with expectation.

"Why has Ned's debt been forgiven? The bitch should pay it."

I wince at him referring to Tory in such a way. "No reason for such language, Father. So far, she's been compliant."

He has no idea.

All the same, the knowledge in my father's words throws me off balance. How? The decision was mine alone, fresh from last night, shared with no one but Tory herself. I scan their faces, seeking a hint, a clue. Nothing. The revelation hangs heavy, an unseen maneuver in a game I thought I controlled.

"Of course she's been compliant – you forgave the debt! For the sum you just brushed away she ought to be painting your goddamn house!"

Frowning, I counter, "She doesn't have the money. She's barely making ends meet, living in the back of the shop." My defense, laying bare Tory's struggles, feels like a betrayal, yet necessary to explain my motivations.

Aleksey jumps in, his voice laced with a solution that's as cold as it is practical. "She can sell the shop. The space is worth more than her debt."

"Someone's done his research," I say, my tone sharp.

"Someone has to work around here," Aleksey counters. "And if the rest of us enforcers went around forgiving debts, there'd be no operation to speak of."

"And how would you afford the premium gas for your tiny-dick car then?" I reply quietly.

Aleksey narrows his eyes, looking practically ready to fight.

"Enough." Father's tone ends the scrap before it can begin. His nod seals my worst fears. "The debt is not erased," he declares, his verdict final, a command that rewrites my intentions, my promises to Tory.

THE ARRANGEMENT | 73

Shit. I'd hope Father would forgive this move. No such luck.

"I've already cleared it with her. The woman's struggling. It's not just about the money," I press, trying to find footing in an argument that seems to be slipping away from me.

Father's response is immediate, his voice cutting through any semblance of debate. "The decision has been made, Maksim. Our word is our bond. You can't just erase debts because you feel pity for someone. Imagine if word were to get out of what you did. Every business in the city would be asking for our mercy."

Sounds like word already did get out, I think, still wondering how the hell my father even knows about this.

"But isn't there a line? Something that separates us from—" I try again, desperate to make him see reason.

"There are no lines when it comes to our business. You know this. The woman will find a way to pay." My father's tone brooks no further argument.

From the corner of my eye, I catch Aleksey's smug expression, a silent testament to his satisfaction with how the conversation is unfolding.

Before I can probe further, before I can dissect the layers of betrayal and secrecy that seem to be wrapping tighter around me, Adelina bursts through the door. Her presence serves as an immediate cease-fire.

"Papa!" she exclaims. "Can we go?"

The argument, the tension, it all fades into the background, pushed aside by the immediacy of her needs. This isn't the time or place to delve deeper into my suspicions.

"Take her," Father says. "She's been looking forward to this since you dropped her off last night."

With a final glance at Father and Aleksey, a silent promise to settle this unfinished business, I turn my attention to Adelina. She moves effortlessly across the room. She plants a soft kiss on Father's cheek, a gesture of affection for her grandfather that momentarily softens the hardened lines of his face.

"Oh, little one," he says, giving her a hug. "You make me feel like a young man again."

She laughs and turns to me, her small hand finding mine with urgency. "I'm starving, Papa," she declares, pulling me back to the present, back to the role that matters most.

"Then I won't keep you waiting another moment. Come."

"Bye *Dedushka*, bye Uncle Alex."

As I allow her to lead me away, I cast one last glance over my shoulder. Aleksey is leaning in close to Father, a conspiratorial whisper shared between them. Even from this distance, even without catching every word, I'm certain I hear Tory's name pass between them.

This moment, fleeting yet loaded with implication, cements the unease that's been building in the pit of my stomach. The argument may have been paused, the immediate confrontation dissolved by Adelina's entrance, but the undercurrents of betrayal and secrecy are far from resolved.

With Adelina's hand in mine, her anticipation for breakfast pulling me forward, I step out of the office, the weight of unresolved tensions pressing heavily on my shoulders. The battle lines are drawn, not just against external threats, but within the very walls that are supposed to be my stronghold.

CHAPTER 12

TORY

Waking up this morning felt like emerging from a fog, especially when I reached out, half-hoping to find Maksim still beside me. But, of course, it was just me, clinging to the lingering scent of him.

But on my desk—a note from him. My irritation melted into a fluttery excitement. Maksim is an enigma, wrapped in a bit of mystery. His words on paper are sweet, but he's all intrigue and hidden depths in person. It's both exasperating and exhilarating.

Lying in bed, holding onto that note, I'm fully immersed in the Maksim experience. He's a blend of mystery and warmth, a man who, despite his shadows, brings a light into my life I'm still trying to comprehend. Lost in these thoughts, I'm genuinely excited about what the future holds.

Getting up, I tuck the note away like it's a treasured secret. Maksim Morozov is a puzzle, complex and intriguing, and I'm more than ready to discover all his hidden facets.

As I'm trying to shake off the sleep and get my day started, I find my mind drifting back to Maksim. Specifically, his voice—there's something about the way he spoke, all firm and commanding, that's stuck with me. In the heat of the moment, him telling me what to do, commanding me... I never pegged myself as someone who'd be into that. But, surprise, surprise, I was *way* into it. It was hot, feeling safe, being tuned into someone else's lead, especially when that someone is as dialed in as Maksim.

There's this rush in letting go, in trusting him enough to take the reins. It felt like I was in these incredibly capable, albeit slightly dangerous, hands. And the more I think about it, the more I realize I'm itching to dive deeper into whatever this is. There's a whole world of experiences Maksim hinted at, and my curiosity's got the better of me. I want in, even though every sensible part of me is waving red flags and warning signs.

But, caution be damned, there's this part of me that's just craving more. More of that control, more of that release. It's a tightrope walk between what I know I should do and what I want to do. And right now, want is winning by a landslide.

So, with that whirlwind of thoughts making a mess of my brain, I hustle to get dressed. It's a new day, and apparently, I've got new interests to contemplate. I'm just smoothing down my shirt when I step out of the office, right on cue to see Nicky walking in, arms loaded with coffees.

Even with the promise of a fresh coffee and the start of a regular day's work ahead, my mind's still half-tangled up with thoughts of Maksim. Thoughts of last night and, if I'm being totally honest, thoughts of what could happen next.

Nicky throws me for a loop. "You know you're not due for another hour, right?"

I can't help but question him, my eyebrows arching up in surprise. "I'm sorry?"

He just grins, setting down a coffee in front of me. "Thought I'd get a jump on the day, you know? Figured I could lend a hand," he explains, all casual like it's just another Tuesday when he's decided to be an early bird.

I'm about to dive into a whole spiel when he's already making tracks to the back, presumably to gear up for the day ahead. So there I am, coffee in hand, a bit stumped. Nicky's a great guy, but I really don't know much about him, beyond the basics and the fact that he's a solid worker.

Shrugging off the confusion, I take a grateful sip of the coffee – Nicky's timing is uncanny; I needed this. Then, it's down to business. I flip open my laptop, pulling up the schedule for the day. A small, relieved smile creeps up on me when I see Howard the Great Dane's name missing from the list. Don't get me wrong, Howard's a sweetheart, but man, his bathroom breaks are something out of a horror movie.

The phone's ringtone pulls me out of my scheduling reverie, and as I make my way to the back office. "Hello, Paws and Play, this is Tory," I answer, still with a half-smile plastered on my face.

"Hi, Tory, it's Ellen. Listen, I'm feeling under the weather today, so Meatball won't be coming in. I'll still cover his day, of course," says one of my regulars, her voice full of sniffles and apologies.

"Oh, Ellen, I'm sorry to hear that! I hope you feel better soon. And don't worry about Meatball. We'll miss him, but your spot's here when you're both ready," I reassure her, slipping into my best caring business owner mode.

"Thanks, Tory. I really appreciate it. See you soon," she replies, a bit of relief in her voice.

"Take care. Get well soon!" I hang up, chuckling softly to myself about the oddities of running a doggy daycare. You get attached, not just to the pets, but their people too.

The sound of the front doors swinging open catches my attention. "Nicky, could you get that?" I call out, expecting to hear his footsteps or at least a shout back. Silence. *Weird.* Shrugging, I wrap up my call log and head out myself to see who's just walked in.

I push through to the main space of the shop, eyes scanning, trying to catch a glimpse of whoever just breezed through the door. But it's like a ghost town – not a soul in sight. And it hits me: no one's scheduled to drop off their pup for another thirty minutes.

After the whole whirlwind with Maksim, I've been religious about locking the front door, a little slice of common sense in my otherwise unpredictable life. But Nicky, bless his heart, must've spaced on that detail. Seriously, where the heck is he?

"Nicky?" I call out again, louder this time, my voice echoing in the empty space. Silence. Not even the echo of my own footsteps for company.

The realization that I'm standing in the quiet shop alone, with the door probably swinging in the wind thanks to

Nicky's oversight, sends a ripple of frustration through me. I make a mental note to have a chat with him about security protocols, about locking doors. But first, I've got to find him. It's not like Nicky to just vanish.

With a sigh, I start a more thorough search, peering behind counters, checking the back rooms, even poking my head into the tiny storage closet that barely fits a vacuum cleaner and a shelf of cleaning supplies. But nada. Nicky's pulled a Houdini on me, and I'm not amused.

"Great, just what I needed today."

As if materializing from the shadows themselves, two men emerge abruptly, seizing my arms with a ferocity that sends waves of shock and terror coursing through me.

"You're coming with us," one of them declares.

The cold certainty in his tone makes it clear this is no random altercation. This is targeted, deliberate, and I'm the focus of their unwelcome attention.

My initial shock morphs into pure adrenaline-fueled resistance. I'm kicking, screaming, thrashing like my life depends on it because it might just. "Nicky! Help!" I yell at the top of my lungs, hoping he's somewhere close, hoping anyone's close.

In the chaos, I manage to sink my teeth into one of the guy's arms, a desperate move that pays off when he yelps in pain and loosens his grip. But my victory is short-lived. In the scuffle, I lose my balance, my head connecting with the sharp edge of the counter. The world goes black before I even hit the ground.

CHAPTER 13

TORY

Waking up with the taste of confusion in my mouth, the first thing I notice is my jaw aching like it's been on the wrong end of a punch. Where the heck am I? My eyes flicker open, taking in the surroundings, and it's definitely not my cozy Murphy bed in the back of the shop.

Panic flutters in my chest as I think about the shop. Did Nicky manage to call Ty? Hell, does he even know I got snatched? What about the police—did anyone think to dial 911? The questions barrel through my mind, each one ramping up my worry.

Trying to sit up causes my head to spin, a lovely dose of dizziness just to spice things up. But I've got to get my bearings. The room's got that bland, sterile feel of an office, but it's plonked right in the middle of some warehouse, all bare concrete and cold steel.

I push myself up, ignoring the merry-go-round in my head, and stagger over to the door. Locked, obviously, because why make my day easy? Dead bolted for that extra touch of "you're not going anywhere."

A quick search is next on the agenda. I'm tearing through desk drawers like a madwoman, half expecting to find a key waving at me with a sign that says 'escape here.' But luck's not on my side—nothing. No key, no helpful tools, not even a paperclip for a makeshift lock-picking attempt.

Stuck in a kidnapper's office décor nightmare, I'm trying to piece together my next move. My brain's doing somersaults, trying to figure out if I can MacGyver my way out of here, but without anything useful in sight, options are looking slim.

My thoughts circle back to the shop, to Nicky, Ty, and even Howard the Great Dane with his monster poops. God, I'd give anything to be dealing with that mess instead of this.

Is this whole business about Ned's loan? I thought Maksim had squared it away, said it was all forgiven. Was that just a line? A play to get me into bed after all? My mind races through the possibilities, each more unsettling than the last.

Then, the sound of the door unlocking snaps me out of my spiraling thoughts. Instinct kicks in, and I'm back in the chair. Whoever is coming in, I'm not taking any chances.

A man I've never seen is standing in the doorway, gazing at me. His expression is strange, and all I can think about are the serial killers I've seen documentaries about. I look around again for a weapon, but I see nothing.

"Who are you? What do you want?" I ask, my voice as steady as I can make it.

He ignores my questions and grabs my arm like we're in some sort of action movie.

I pull away, my anger flaring. "Don't touch me!" I snap, my patience fraying at the edges.

"Shut up," he hisses, his grip tightening as he pushes me toward the door and down the hallway. I'm screaming my head off, hoping a decent person might be somewhere in the building and hear me. It's not doing me a damn bit of good, however – this place is so bleak and endless that I might as well be at the bottom of the ocean.

We reach another door and the man knocks.

"What is this?" I ask. "What's going on?"

"Didn't you hear me when I said *shut up?*"

Before our conversation can go on any further, the door opens. Inside the room, like some bad cliche, stand two thugs. I don't know them from Adam, but it's clear they're not here to exchange pleasantries.

What in the world is going on? My brain's trying to connect the dots, but it's like trying to solve a puzzle in the dark. So many questions, zero answers, and here I am, being manhandled out of a room by some stranger.

I'm sizing up the duo who have apparently decided to crash my not-so-glamorous kidnapping. One has that youthful, I-think-I'm-tough vibe, probably clocks in somewhere in his thirties. He's wearing gold rings on three of his fingers, and the top buttons of his shirt is undone to show off the ink on his chest. The flash of cockiness in his smile makes me instantly want to wipe it off his face. His eyes are hidden behind big, gaudy Dior sunglasses.

The other guy is older, a little plump, dressed in a dark suit, his silver hair slicked back, his face impassive. Not a doubt in my mind he's the one in charge.

The other man walks back the way we came, leaving me with Tweedledee and Tweedledum, I can't help but let out a snort. This whole situation would be hilarious if it weren't so utterly messed up.

I look at the two men and decide to address the older man. My eyes fixed on him, I ask, "What's going on here? Why am I here?" Neither man answers my questions, and I'm not sure what to do. So I wait in silence, hoping they'll eventually tell me what's going on.

The younger guy steps forward, all swagger, and introduces himself. "I'm Aleksey Morozov," he says, placing his fingertip on his chest, that smirk never leaving his lips. With a grand gesture like he's presenting a prize on a game show, he points to the older man, "And this is Igor Morozov."

Igor, for his part, might as well be a statue, offering me nothing but a silent, evaluating stare. But damn, if he doesn't have that same Morozov vibe—like an older, grizzled version of Maksim. The pieces click into place, confirming my suspicion that I've somehow landed in the middle of a Russian mob drama.

Igor finally speaks, his voice deep and unforgiving. "You owe me one hundred thousand dollars."

"Maksim said he cleared the debt."

Aleksey's quick to jump in, his cocky smile turning into a smirk. "Maksim is not in a position to make that decision."

Aleksey's looking at me like I'm the next item on his to-do list, and Igor—well, he's just staring, probably trying to intimidate me into submission.

"Look, I don't know what kind of business you think this is, but it has nothing to do with me. Ned borrowed that money, not me. And for the record, Maksim assured me we were square." I cross my arms, doing my best to project confidence I don't feel. I don't have the money, I can't pay them, so I'm not sure what to do here.

Aleksey glances at Igor, speaking in Russian I don't understand. Igor remains impassive.

"What was that?" I ask.

"Just commenting on your little arrangement with Maksim," Aleksey says. "You two came to a nice *agreement*, yes?"

"What the hell are you implying?"

"You're a smart woman, I'm sure you'll figure it out."

"You fu-"

Igor raises his hand, silencing us both with his obvious authority. "Enough." The word drops like a lead ball onto the ground.

Standing there, trying to muster all the toughness I possess, a tiny crack forms in my armor. The thought of Maksim playing me, using lies to get me into bed, slices right through me. I'm boiling with anger—at him, at myself for getting swept up in his world, his charm. How could I have been so naive?

"I'm telling you, I don't have it," I repeat, my voice steady, though it's a struggle to keep it from wavering.

Igor, with all the warmth of a Siberian winter, drops another bombshell on me. "If you sold your shop, you could settle your debt."

The very idea has me reeling. "Not happening," I shoot back, trying to sound more defiant than desperate.

But Aleksey isn't having any of it. He leans in, his threat thinly veiled. "You might not have a choice. It'd be a shame if something happened to your shop. Insurance could take care of your problem too."

My heart's hammering against my chest. Fear, raw and unyielding, takes hold. They're cornering me, ready to rip away everything I've worked for. My shop, my sanctuary, could be reduced to ashes just to satisfy their greed.

The reality of my situation crashes over me—I'm out of my depth here, facing a tidal wave ready to sweep away my entire life.

Panic knots in my stomach. What am I supposed to do against the might of the Morozovs? They're not just going to go away, and I can't conjure up the money they demand. They're ready to destroy everything to get what they want, and I'm powerless to stop them.

Just as despair threatens to drown me, the door slams open with the force of a storm. Maksim strides in, fury etched in every line of his body, a bag clenched in his fist. The air shifts, charged with his anger, and for a moment, everything else fades away.

My heart's caught between hope and fear, not knowing what his next move will be.

CHAPTER 14

MAKSIM

The moment I see Tory, seated and vulnerable, something snaps inside me—a fury, raw and consuming, unlike anything I've felt before. Every instinct screams to tear Aleksey apart, to reduce him to nothing with my bare hands for what he's done. Yet I clamp down on that urge, keeping the beast at bay. Control is everything in moments like these.

When I see the bruise on her face, the rage returns.

I want blood, family or not.

I point directly at Tory's bruise, my voice a blade. "Who did this?" The demand is for my father, but Aleksey steps forward, the hint of a challenge in his stance.

"I did," he confesses, brazen and unrepentant. "You were too slow to act, Maksim. I took initiative." His words are like gasoline on the inferno raging inside me.

My gaze shifts to my father, searching for a sign, any indication that this isn't sanctioned. But the slight nod he gives confirms my worst fears—he allowed this to happen.

"Spying on me, Aleksey?" I probe further, the question laced with ice.

As I confront the chaos before me, Tory tries to edge in, her voice a whisper against the storm. "Maksim, I—"

Aleksey cuts her off, his voice booming, overriding hers with an arrogance that sets my teeth on edge. "This isn't about her, Maksim. It's about us, about our family and how we handle business. Something you seem to have forgotten how to do."

Her attempt to speak, though swiftly silenced, strikes a chord within me. The sight of her, trying to find her voice amidst this power struggle, ignites a protective fury deep in my chest.

"The hell it isn't about her," I snap back, my focus narrowing on Tory's bruised form. "You bring her into this, hurt her, and attempt to claim it's about family honor? She is under my protection."

The room falls silent for a moment, the weight of my declaration hanging heavy in the air. Tory's eyes meet mine, a mix of pain and something fiercer shining back. In that gaze, I find my resolve.

The realization hits hard—I am embroiled in a war not with my enemies but with my own blood. Aleksey's actions, sanctioned by Igor, aren't just an assault on Tory; they're a direct challenge to me, to my authority, my decisions. A declaration that my loyalty, divided as it is, must now choose a side.

Aleksey, with his reckless ambition, has just escalated this from a family dispute to a battle line drawn in the sand.

Tory's injury hardens my resolve. I will shield her from further harm, even if it means standing against my own flesh and blood. The game has changed, and with it, so must I.

Aleksey's smugness is palpable, his every word dripping with contempt. Father watches us like we're pieces on his chessboard, his expression unreadable but keenly observant. The air between us crackles with tension, a prelude to the storm about to break.

"We're running a business here, Maksim," Aleksey starts, his tone patronizing, as if explaining the obvious to a child. "A hundred grand isn't pocket change to just write off because you got distracted by a pretty face." He leans in, a vile smirk playing on his lips, "And let's be clear, she can't settle her debts in bed. This isn't about whatever fling you're having. It's cash we're after. Getting your rocks off with this little whore is a distraction we don't need."

His words ignite something fierce within me, a surge of protectiveness and anger that narrows my vision to just Aleksey and the space between us. Without thinking, I lunge at him, a growl of rage escaping my lips.

Before I can reach him, Father's command cuts through the tension. "Enough!" He snaps his fingers, and like magic, three of his goons barrel into the room, pulling me back and putting themselves between us.

I'm seething, shaking with the effort it takes to hold myself back. The goons have their hands on me, but I shrug them off, stepping back to regain my composure. I realize then that brute force won't win this battle.

Breathing hard, I lock eyes with my father, trying to convey a message beyond words. This isn't over. Not by a long shot.

"This isn't just about money, and you know it," I say, my voice steady despite the adrenaline pumping through my veins. "This is about respect, about decency. Something you both seem to have forgotten."

My father remains silent, his gaze shifting from me to Aleksey, who's still looking smug even in the hold of the goons. It's clear he's considering the situation, weighing his next move.

Aleksey, undeterred by his brief moment of restraint, scoffs as he shakes the men loose. "Decency? In our line of work? You're delusional, brother. She owes us, and she'll pay, one way or another."

My anger toward Aleksey simmers beneath the surface, a raging inferno held in check by sheer willpower. I catch Tory's eye, her own fury mirroring mine, especially after Aleksey's crude insinuation. A quick nod from me, a silent message that now's not the time for vengeance, seems to calm her just a bit. But make no mistake, Aleksey's words have marked him in both our eyes.

My brother, unfazed by our silent exchange, continues with his provocation. "You should be thankful, Maksim, that there are those in this family who understand how to properly run a business," he says, cockiness lacing every word.

I'm about to snap once more, to put him in his place, when Father's voice, deep and commanding, cuts through the tension.

"Enough!" he bellows once more, his voice booming through the room. "This bickering is pointless. The debt is what brought us here."

"Yes, the money," I echo, my voice laced with a controlled anger. It's time to end this charade, to bring this confrontation to a conclusion. I turn to the leather bag I'd brought with me, now on the floor, its contents the answer to the standoff we find ourselves in.

"You want your money? Here it is," I declare, my tone leaving no room for further debate. I grab the bag, tossing it directly at Aleksey. He catches it, surprise flickering across his face for a moment before it's quickly masked by his usual arrogance.

The room falls silent, the only sound the rustle of cash as Aleksey opens the bag to confirm its contents. Father watches closely, his expression unreadable, while Tory, silent, stands with a strength that speaks volumes.

Aleksey looks between the cash and me, a glimmer of understanding passing through his gaze. "This changes nothing," he finally says, but the edge in his voice has softened, if only slightly. "You still broke protocol, went over our father's head for that woman."

I laugh, knowing he's desperate, grasping at straws. "You said it was all about the money, did you not?" I gesture towards the bag. "There it is. What difference does it make where it came from?"

"And what if it's not all there?" Aleksey protests, his weakest gambit yet. "We should count it."

I snort. "Bill me if I'm short."

Aleksey's jaw is working. He's not happy with the way this turned out at all. But that's no matter. He can squirm and pout all he wants.

I turn to my father. "I'll be over later. We need to talk more thoroughly about this whole mess," I say, my gaze unwavering, challenging him to disagree.

For a moment, my father meets my stare, the silent exchange thick with unspoken words. Then, with a slight nod, he concedes.

Without another word, I turn to Tory. Our eyes meet, and in hers, I see a mix of questions, fear, and a trust that humbles me. Her trust steels my resolve as I take her hand.

"Come on, let's get you out of here," I tell her, the words low but filled with a protective firmness. I pull her to her feet, my grip reassuring, as we make our way out of the warehouse, leaving the weight of the confrontation behind us.

CHAPTER 15

TORY

As Maksim yanks me through the labyrinth of the factory, my feet barely touching the ground, I let out a stream of protests.

"Hey! I'm not some little doll you can just cart around whenever you feel like it," I snap, trying to wiggle free from his iron grip.

Maksim quiets me with a command so sharp, so utterly bold, it's like hitting a mute button on my defiance. "Enough."

I'm silent, a surprising thrill running through me at his authoritative tone. I'm not used to men speaking to me like this, and it's disconcerting how much I find myself responding to it. There's something about the way Maksim takes charge that's unsettling and attractive, even if my inner feminist is screaming objections.

Before I know it, we're at his car—a sleek, luxury beast that looks like it eats miles for breakfast. Despite everything,

Maksim takes the time to guide me into the seat with care, as if I'm the most precious cargo imaginable.

The silence envelops us as we drive away, my thoughts swirling uncontrollably. The realization hits me hard; Maksim didn't clear my debt as some twisted seduction tactic. His coming to my rescue, standing up against his own flesh and blood, and it speaks volumes. He's in this for reasons I can't fully understand, but what's clear is his intentions are not filled with manipulation or deceit.

The ride is quiet, the kind of silence that's thick with unspoken words and lingering tension. I steal glances at him, trying to decipher the man behind the wheel. Maksim's focus is unyielding, his jaw set in determination.

As we glide through the city, the silence stretches between us, thick with unspoken questions and half-formed thoughts. My mind's racing, trying to piece together the events that led us here. The more I think about it, the more one question burns brighter than the rest: How did Maksim even know I was in trouble?

Gathering my courage, I turn toward him. "Maksim, how did you know I needed help?"

There's a pause, a moment where he seems to weigh his words carefully before he answers. "I had cameras installed in your office and the front of your business," he admits, his voice tinged with hesitation.

Shock courses through me, a cocktail of disbelief and violation that's hard to swallow. Before I can fully process this intrusion, another, far more embarrassing realization dawns on me. Did he witness my most private moments?

"You saw...everything?" My voice is a mix of horror and curiosity, hardly louder than a whisper. "I mean, *everything* everything?" There's no doubt what I'm referring to.

Another few beats pass.

"Yes, I did," he responds, the regret in his voice unmistakable. "And I'm sorry. That wasn't my intention."

His apology hangs in the air, a confession that unexpectedly shifts something within me. Here I am, supposed to be outraged, yet part of me can't help but acknowledge the complexity of his actions. It's a bizarre feeling, knowing he's seen me at my most vulnerable, yet it's his straightforward admission and evident remorse that softens the blow.

As the cityscape blurs past us, my emotions are a tangled mess. I should be furious, and part of me is. Yet, there's another part, confusingly touched by his protective instincts, however misguidedly executed.

"Okay," I finally say, the word more an acknowledgment of his honesty than forgiveness. "But you will take them down immediately, understand?"

He lets out a halfhearted chuckle, the tension easing just a fraction. "Of course."

The weight of Maksim's admission hangs heavy in the car, a tangled mix of embarrassment and anger knotting in my stomach. His silence, thick with what I can only guess is shame, does little to ease the turmoil churning inside me.

"Take me back to my shop," I demand, the words sharp, cutting through the tension. After that, I retreat into silence.

Out of the corner of my eye, I watch him open his mouth. Maybe he wants to say another word in his defense. But whatever is on his mind, he closes his mouth, shaking his head.

He's paid my debt, a fact that keeps replaying in my mind. But it strikes me, hard—wasn't that debt imposed on me unfairly to begin with? My emotions are a whirlwind, gratitude mingling with resentment, relief shadowed by a deep-seated anger for the privacy he's stolen from me.

The realization that Maksim, for all his protective gestures, is entangled in a world fraught with betrayal, leaves me reeling. Knowing he's associated with people who wouldn't think twice about harming others adds a layer of fear to the already complicated mess of my feelings.

Rationally, I should want to sever all ties with him. To run as far from his dangerous world as I can get. Yet, despite the chaos, despite the fear and the violation of my privacy, there's an undeniable pull that I can't ignore. My body betrays me, craving his presence, his touch, even as my mind screams caution.

The silence stretches on, a chasm filled with unasked questions and unresolved emotions. The more I think about it, the more conflicted I feel. Grateful for his intervention, yet furious for the intrusion. Terrified by the danger his life represents, yet inexplicably drawn to him. It's a paradox I can't seem to resolve.

As we drive, a suspicion starts to worm its way into my thoughts—we're definitely not headed back to my shop. The silence between us is thick, charged with all the things left unsaid, until I can't take it anymore.

"Hey, where do you think you're taking me? Drop me off," I demand.

Maksim's response is frustratingly calm. "I just want a chance to talk, to explain. We're going to my place—just for a bit." He adds, with a hint of something that might be concern. "And I need to ensure my father's truly going to back off. You'll be safe there."

I let out a sigh, half irritation, half resignation. Sure, part of me is curious to hear what he's got to say, and the other part —the one that's not keen on being a mob target—admits that a confirmation of being out of danger wouldn't be the worst thing.

"Ty's probably flipping out wondering where I've vanished to."

He offers his phone to me, an olive branch. I eye it, fighting the impulse to knock it out of his hand in a fit of defiance. But as much as I want to stick it to him and demand he turn the car around this instant, a bigger part of me is dying to hear his side of the story. After all, Maksim's not the one who got me into this mess; that honor goes to Ned, and that guy's not around to answer for his sins.

"Alright, give it here," I grumble, taking his phone. Might as well let Ty know I haven't been abducted by aliens or run off to join the circus—not yet, anyway.

As I dial Ty's number, I feel like I'm walking a tightrope between my fierce need for independence and the unsettling realization that Maksim, in his own twisted way, might just have my back. It's a weird place to be, caught between wanting to throttle him and wanting to hear him out.

As the phone rings, I rehearse a quick explanation in my head, something to smooth over my unexpected absence without causing a panic.

"Hey, Ty, it's me," I start, trying to sound calmer than I feel. "Had a bit of an emergency. Everything okay at the shop?"

Ty's voice is a balm to my frayed nerves. "Yeah, got a call from our first client on my cell. Made it there in time, so no issues. What's up? You alright?"

I let out a breath I didn't realize I was holding. "Yeah, I'm good. Glad to hear you were able to cover. Thank you. Today's a slow day, thankfully. I'll be back soon and fill you in on all the drama."

"Drama! I am intrigued!" he replies with a relieved laugh. "I'm just glad you're all right. See you later."

"Thanks, Ty." Hanging up, I hand the phone back to Maksim. "Thanks for letting me use your phone. And for... this, I guess." I gesture vaguely between us, the car, the road – this whole bizarre detour my day has taken.

Maksim takes his phone back, a hint of something like gratitude in his gaze. "Thank you for giving me a chance to explain," he says, and it's sincere enough to tug at the edges of my resolve.

But as we drive, I wonder if I'm trading one mess for another? Sure, Maksim stepped up, played the hero when I needed one. But the more I think about it, the more I question whether his rescue comes with strings attached. Is this just trading one kind of trouble for another?

"Look," I start, turning to face him fully, "pulling me out of the fire with those two? That's on the plus side. But don't think I'm not weighing my options here. Getting involved with you... it's like hopping from the frying pan into the fire."

He nods, a wry smile playing at his lips. "Understood. But let me try to even the scales a bit, okay?"

I settle back into my seat, crossing my arms as I mull over his words. Part of me is ready to bolt, to get as far from Maksim Morozov and his complicated world as possible. But there's another part, curious and undeniably drawn to the man beside me, that wants to give him a chance.

"Fine," I say finally, "but it better be one hell of an explanation."

We're soon cruising through a part of Chicago that looks like it leapt straight out of a "Lifestyles of the Rich and Famous" episode. Each house we pass is more eye-popping than the last, making my quaint shop apartment feel more like a cardboard box by comparison.

His house is big and classy, with all the quiet confidence of a Broadway star knowing they're about to nail their performance. The kind of house that doesn't need to brag, because one look at its tasteful architecture and perfectly manicured lawns does all the talking.

Maksim stops the car, and I'm just staring out the window, thinking, *Girl, what have you gotten yourself into?* Marching into Maksim's lair feels a bit like willingly walking into a beautifully decorated trap.

"Seriously? You live in this palace?" I ask, unable to keep the awe out of my voice.

Maksim cracks a smile, clearly amused by my reaction. "Welcome to my home."

Following him to the door, I shake my head in disbelief. Stepping into his world, even just for a bit, feels like crossing into uncharted territory. Here I am, about to dive headfirst into the opulence, fully aware that I'm out of my element.

CHAPTER 16

MAKSIM

As we stride through the grandiose halls of my home, I catch glimpses of surprise and admiration in Tory's eyes. Her curiosity piques as we move deeper into the house.

"So all this room for just you and your daughter?" she inquires, scanning the surroundings that likely seem worlds apart from what she's accustomed to.

"Not exactly," I reply, a trace of warmth seeping into my voice. "Irina, our live-in nanny, lives here as well, though they are both out at the moment."

The mention of my daughter and a nanny sparks a reaction in Tory. She hesitates, then ventures, "It's kind of hard to picture you as a dad." She hurries to clarify, her gaze dropping to my hands—hands that have known violence. "I mean no offense. It's just that..."

I understand the unspoken words hanging between us. The hands she's looking at have protected, fought, and done what was necessary to keep my world intact. But they're also the hands that hold my daughter close, wipe away her tears, and carry her when she's too tired to walk.

"No offense taken," I assure her, catching her gaze with my own. "There's more to me than meets the eye, Tory. Being a father is the most important part of who I am."

The moment feels significant, a bridge of understanding being cautiously constructed between us. It's clear that Tory's view of me is evolving, grappling with the complexities of a man who operates in the shadows yet shines brightest in the light of his daughter's love.

As we continue the tour, I'm acutely aware of the shift in the air, the subtle dance of revelations and realizations playing out between us. Tory's presence in the heart of my home feels like a step into uncharted territory—a blending of worlds that until now I kept meticulously separate.

Once we're settled in the expansive confines of my study, a room that's seen many a late night and early morning, I offer Tory a drink.

"Water okay?" I ask, already heading towards the decanter to pour two glasses.

"Water's fine," she confirms, her voice steady, betraying none of the whirlwind I suspect is tearing through her thoughts. I nod, mirroring her choice, and hand her a glass before taking my seat opposite her.

The wingback chairs, usually reserved for solitary reflections or intense discussions, now frame this unexpected dialogue between us.

I'm well aware of what needs to be said, the assurances I must give to quell the storm I've unwittingly drawn her into.

But finding the right words feels like navigating a minefield, especially with Tory sitting there, an image of casual allure in her tight jeans and form-fitting top. The seriousness of our conversation wars with the distraction she presents.

Part of me wants to take her, to ravage her once again, to bite her neck, to claim her. But I quell the animal urges raging in me. I might be in the mood, but no doubt she's still scared after what happened to her.

"I want you to know," I begin, steeling myself for the conversation ahead, "you won't have to deal with Igor or Aleksey again. They'll stay out of your life."

Tory listens, her expression a duality of skepticism and hope. The silence stretches between us before she voices a concern that's clearly been weighing on her. "Maksim, I'm not sure I can live in your world. It's too much."

"You don't have to live my life to be with me," I reply, earnestness coloring my tone. "All I ask is for a chance to show you that what we could have can stand apart from the chaos."

The silence is thick with Tory's doubts—about me, my life, and what it means for her. But deep down, I know she's the one, even if it's too soon to say it out loud. That certainty is like a pulse inside me, strong and undeniable.

She shifts in her seat, her eyes flicking toward the fire. She wrings her hands, and I can sense there is much on her mind, much she doesn't know how to even begin to say.

I lean over and take her hand. The sensation of her skin against mine is electrifying, as always. My heart beats faster as I hold her small palm in mine.

God, the things I want to do to her.

"Tell me what's on your mind."

"Where to even start?" She brings her gaze to mine. "You're a mobster. How about starting there?"

"I am. I'm a criminal."

Her eyes flash, suggesting she hadn't expected me to be so straightforward. If her ex is any indication, she's likely used to deceit.

She shakes her head. "I don't know. When I was dating Ned, I knew he was a crook, a bad guy. But I guess I was able to write it off, like it was some little quirk, or a hobby or something. I knew he wasn't big time. Didn't hurt people."

I say nothing, letting her say everything she needs to say.

"But you... you're not some guy who runs favors for the mob for a little extra cash and some bragging rights. You're clearly much more involved than that." Her gaze drifts over the room, as if my life can be summed up by the wealth that surrounds us.

"I suppose you could say that."

"And I'm guessing you're in it for life. Not like Ned."

Ned *had* been in it for life, in a matter of speaking. But I understand her point.

"Yes. Ever since I was a boy in Moscow. This is the only world I've known."

"And what's going to happen? Where is this *career* of yours going to end up?"

She has no idea what she's broached with this topic. The question of just who is to take the reins of the Bratva when my father passes or steps down is a point of contention in the family. I, as the eldest, am the front-runner. Not to mention the little detail that I can actually run a business, unlike Aleksey.

Aleksey knows this, knows that it's only a matter of time until my father announces me as the heir. But until then, he's keeping his mouth shut – one of the few wise decisions he's ever made. But there's no doubt that the fallout will be intense when my father finally makes the call. My half-brother isn't the type of man to take bad news well.

But Tory doesn't need to know any of this. It's "inside baseball," as the Americans like to say.

"It's not official yet," I say. "But my father is likely to name me the heir. He's not exactly the retiring type, however. So it will be a good long while until I take the reins."

She shifts in her seat. "Then you're going to be the boss."

"I'm going to be the boss."

A sigh. "You know, there's a time when the idea of dating the head of the Russian mob would've been a hell of a turn-on. But now that I'm looking down the barrel of it..." she trails off.

I can't resist. "You mean it's *not* a turn-on?" I follow my words with a small smile.

Her eyes flash, her mouth forming a hard line. "That's not the point!"

I chuckle. "I see what you're saying. Life with me would be outside of the law."

"Right."

"It's a risk, I'm not going to lie. I've put in my time, however, paid my dues. My *hands-on* days are long behind me. Day to day, my life is more like that of a businessman."

"Except when you're shaking down people for money."

"The personal touch is occasionally necessary."

She bites her lower lip in thought, and damned if it isn't sexy as hell.

"*Hands on...* does that mean you've killed people?" She challenges me with her gaze.

"I appreciate directness." But how to reply to her question? The answer is *yes*, of course. The objective in this conversation is not to scare her, however. "Let's just say my past is long behind me."

She shifts in her seat. Tory's a smart woman; the implication in my phrasing is obvious.

"Right. Okay." She's processing. I say nothing.

"The way we met," I went on. "That's the most direct I am these days. I typically have underlings handle such matters, but now and then the hand of the *vor* can expedite certain processes."

Another sigh, another shake of her head. After a few beats, she gets up and makes her way over to the fire, the glass of water held by the tips of her fingers. She places her other hand on the mantle.

"I just need to know that I'm going to be safe," she says finally. "I can't be involved with a man who makes it necessary to be looking over my shoulder constantly."

I rise, stepping over to her where she stands before the fire. Tory looks so small, so delicate, so innocent. It's strange – I've only known her strength, which she has in abundance. Seeing her like that stirs something in me, something fierce and protective.

I place my hand on her chin, turning her toward me. "I swear, Tory." The words are a whisper against her lips, a vow made in the most intimate of whispers. "I'll protect you. As long as you're in my life, in this world, I'll do whatever it takes to keep you safe. No matter what."

The urge to kiss her is overwhelming, a yearning that's become impossible to ignore. Despite every intention to keep a sliver of distance, to maintain some semblance of restraint, it all crumbles the moment our eyes lock. I lean in, the space between us charged with a magnetic pull that neither of us can deny.

So I don't resist any longer.

Our lips meet in a kiss that's both a promise and a surrender. It's gentle at first, an exploration. But quickly, it deepens, fueled by the emotions swirling between us. Tory responds with equal fervor, her arms wrapping around me, pulling me closer.

She tastes like heaven, her tongue moving over mine, her flavor intoxicating. My hands fall to her hips, and I squeeze the roundness of her curves, pulling her against my hardness. She gasps as she feels my cock. I'm stiff as steel, my cock grinding against her thigh as I show her how much I want her without speaking the words.

The kiss goes on. I grab the hem of her shirt, pulling it up and over her shoulders, the firelight flickering against her perfect body. She resists nothing, instead drawing closer to me with every bite that I take. Her skin is soft and warm as my hands travel up her bare lower back, coming to a stop at the clasp of her bra. I unhook it quickly, and she does the rest, sliding the straps down her lovely shoulders and letting her breasts fall out.

I step back and take in the sight of her topless. Her tits are perfect, round and pert, her nipples rose-pink. Leaning down, I take one into my mouth, teasing it with my tongue.

"Oh... fuck yes," she moans, throwing her head back and holding my head in place.

I make a mental note to make sure I explore every bit of her body in this fashion.

I rise again, gazing at her. All I want is to claim her, to show her how much I want to make her mine, all mine.

Now's not the time for such predilections, I realize. Just as Tory needs to be eased into my life as a *vor*, she'll need to be eased into my tastes in the bedroom.

All the same, I can't resist giving in, just a little.

"Take of your jeans." My words come out in a stern command.

Her eyes flash. "Just like that?"

"Just like that."

"Bossy."

"Comes with the territory."

A small smirk crosses her lips. But as her hands move to the front of her jeans, I know I've gotten my way.

I always do.

Her eyes on mine, she slowly undoes the button of her jeans, then the zipper. Her hands move to her sides, and she begins shimmying down the skin-tight denim, revealing the black panties underneath. I watch her slowly, watch her expose more of her ripe, flawless legs.

The jeans are soon at her ankles, and she steps out of them, moving closer to me.

My blood is growing hot, my hands clenching and unclenching at the sight of Tory nearly nude before me. It takes all the restraint I have to maintain my composure.

Part of me wants to totally let go, to pounce on her like the animal I feel like in those moments.

"Get on your knees."

She bites her lip again, as if she wants to throw some sass in my direction, but she doesn't. Instead, she obeys my command, dropping to her knees in front of me. She looks up, and I once more take her chin into my hand.

"Open my pants."

Tory's gaze falls to my cock, my hardness tenting the fabric of my slacks. She places her hand on me, moving her fingertips slowly over my length, as if she wants to make sure it's actually there. Then she opens my pants, the metal of my buckle clanging just a bit as she undoes it, then my button, then my zipper. She tugs down the black, skin-tight fabric of my boxer-briefs, my cock leaping out in front of her.

She licks her lips.

"Tell me," I say, taking her chin and tilting her head up to me. "How does the sight of my cock make you feel? Does it make you wet?"

She swallows, her gaze drifting down to my manhood.

"Keep your eyes on me."

She obeys.

"Now, tell me."

"Yes, it makes me wet."

"How wet."

"So wet."

"Reach down. Find out how wet it's made you."

Her hand drifts down to the waist band of her panties. I watch carefully as her fingers disappear beneath the black fabric. Soon her hand is between her legs.

"Tell me."

"I'm soaked for you."

"Good. Now, keep your hand there, and give me what we both want."

She returns her attention to my cock, her hand still working between her thighs. She moans slightly, closing her eyes for a moment before refocusing her attention. Tory moves her lips closer, grasping the base of my cock with one hand and placing her lips at the head.

A lick begins the process, gentle but firm enough to send a flash of pleasure up and down my length. She licks me again and again, using a little more pressure each time, as if she knows just what I like.

I place my hand on her cheek, her skin soft and smooth and cool, guiding her down gently. She complies with my wordless instruction, opening her mouth and taking me inside, my head vanishing first, then the first few inches of my shaft.

Part of me wants to bring her down further, but I resist. A mere taste is enough for now.

She wraps her lips around my shaft, her tongue caressing my head.

"Look up at me."

Tory does, the sight of her mouth full of my cock just perfect. Her lips slide back up, then down again. The soft sucking noises of her at work blend with the crackle of the fire, the pleasure becoming more insistent.

Her hand follows her mouth along my length, and I can feel the stirrings of orgasm. But I'm not ready to be done so soon. I stop her, Tory's eyes flicking back to me.

"Get up. Turn around."

She rises, wiping her mouth with the back of her hand, stepping over to the mantle and grasping it with both hands.

"Good girl."

CHAPTER 17

TORY

I'm filled with delicious anticipation as I stand in front of the fire. Maksim is behind me, pacing back and forth slowly, the sound of his dress shoes on the parquet floor echoing through the expanse of the study.

The heat from the flames warms my front. But truth be told, the real heat is between my legs. Maksim's cock was... *delicious*. I licked my lips, savoring the last traces of his taste, that salty, lingering flavor from his pre-cum. I'd wanted to drain him on the spot, but clearly, he had other things in mind for me.

"Take your panties down."

A wave of nervous, excited energy rushes through me at his command. What the hell is it about how bossy Maksim that turns me on so much? I can think about that later. For now, I hook my thumbs underneath the sides of my panties and slide them down slowly. They drop to my ankles and I kick them aside.

The heavy footfalls of Makism's feet draw nearer. He's taking his time, building the anticipation. Finally, he arrives behind me. His big arm wraps around my waist, and he pulls me closer to him. His fingertips move slowly up my back, causing goosebumps to break out. His hands move around, and he cups my breasts, squeezing them gently, just the way I want.

"Tell me what you desire." His voice is low and sensual, but with an animal edge.

"You."

"You need to be more specific than that, my dear."

I grin. He doesn't like to make it easy. "I want you inside me."

Without a word, he places his right hand on mine, bringing it around. Maksim places it on his cock and I gasp. He's so hard, so thick, still wet from my oral work. I stroke him slowly, my chest rising and falling from my heaving breaths.

When I can't take it any longer, when I start guiding him inside, he stops at my entrance.

"Ask for it. Ask me nicely."

I smile, hating it but loving it all at the same time. "Please. *Please*."

"*Please* what?"

My eyes flash with realization. This is it, just like my fantasy. I knew the word he wanted to hear. But how did he know? Sure, he'd had a camera in my office, but he hadn't had one in my head.

Maybe I just knew Maksim better than I'd thought.

I take a deep breath, the words forming on my lips. "Please, sir."

The tension in his body releases, and he lets me guide him inside. I gasp softly at the sensation, his head spreading my lips, pushing slowly, deeply into me. I squirm against him, shoving my ass back, taking him all the way inside me.

There's nothing like the feeling of Maksim's thick, hard cock pushing deep. I let go, bringing my hand to the mantle and gripping it as tightly as I can. It feels insanely good to have him plunging inside, but there's just *so much of him.*

Finally, he bottoms out. I can feel his front pressed against my ass, and his hands move to my hips. He grabs me, making me feel so small in the best way possible. Maksim pulls back and pushes inside, my walls gripping him tightly.

I can't get over the way everything is just on another level with Maksim. The roughness of his hands, the animal grunts that explode from him with each thrust, the way his musk wraps around me. It feels better than good, better than anything.

"I can feel you squeezing me," he says, still plunging inside. "Such a good girl the way you take me."

I moan, pressing my ass harder into him, as if there's a bit of his cock I haven't yet taken.

Already, I can sense the tight coiling of an orgasm deep inside. Maksim's splitting me in half over and over, and if it weren't for his massive arm wrapped around my middle, I'm sure my weakening leg would've buckled underneath me.

I can't resist any longer. The climax breaks and I let out a cry that fills the study. Maksim pulls me close, making sure his manhood is buried to the root as I come, making sure I feel every inch of him. The orgasm fades and he slides out of me – I miss him instantly.

"Did that feel good?" he asks.

"So fucking good."

"I'm glad to hear it."

I can tell there's more. Maksim has an unmistakable edge to his voice, as if I'm some low-level thug working for him who's screwed up. Have I screwed up?

"There's only one problem."

"There is?"

"Mhmm. You didn't ask for permission to come."

I giggle, taking my hands off the mantle and beginning to turn around. "Couldn't hold it back any longer."

"Stop right there." His words freeze me mid-turn. "Put your hands back on the mantle."

His tone is so uncompromising I can't help but obey. Silence hangs in the air as I wait for his next words.

"You were a bad girl, my dear. A very *plokhaya devushka*." Something about his Russian makes his words hit even harder. "You came without my permission, didn't you?"

"I did."

"Thank you for your honesty. But to tell the truth, your confession is necessary. I could tell you were coming just by the way you moaned as I was buried deep inside you, the way your pussy gripped my cock."

A thrill of arousal flashes through me at his words.

"Bad girls get punished, yes? Tell me, are you ready for your punishment?"

I close my eyes, savoring his words. "Yes. Yes, I am."

"Good."

From his position behind me, I feel his big hand cup my right cheek. Then, before I can react, he pulls his hand back and brings it down, the *crack* of skin on skin filling the air. The sting is shocking. It's not even pain, it's pleasure tinged with just enough edge to make it interesting.

"Have you learned your lesson?" he asks.

I'm not sure how to respond, to be honest. Part of me *wants* him to spank me again. "I don't know."

He chuckles. "I'll take that as I no. That is understandable – some lessons need a bit more instruction to settle in one's mind."

His hand moves to my other cheek and, just like before, he lifts his hand and smacks my ass again. The sensation is somehow even more delightful than before.

"I think that did the trick," he says.

I hear the rustling of clothing behind me and glance over my shoulder to see that he's bare.

God, Maksim is sexy. His body is big and powerful, his shoulders round, his chest stout, and his abs showing just enough to turn me on. His chest is dusted with silver hair, and as he turns to make his way toward one of the wingback chairs, my eyes latch onto his perfect, sculpted ass, the muscles moving hypnotically with every step.

He takes a seat on the chair, his cock pointing straight up. The sight is absolutely mouthwatering.

"Come over here," he says, his heated gaze locked onto mine. "Come over here and sit on my cock."

How the hell am I supposed to resist an invitation like that? Then again, with Maksim, they're not invitations – they're orders. And they're orders I'm happy to obey.

I turn around, my ass still throbbing deliciously from the spanks. I make my way over to him, his legs spread slightly, his cock pointing up, and he looks like the emperor of the goddamn world.

When reach him, I spread my legs and begin to straddle him, his cock thick and hard. Before I can lower myself onto him, however, he stops me. Maksim grabs my hip with one hand and puts the other between my legs. He touches my pussy, teasing my clit and making me moan. I close my eyes and focus on the precise sensation of his fingertip against my clit, expertly making slow circles.

"Does that feel good, *plokhaya devushka?*" I don't need to speak Russian to have figured out what these words mean – *bad girl.*

"So fucking good."

"Don't let that fool you. This is part of the punishment. I can tell you want to come."

He's right, but the way he's touching me is too intense to even speak.

"You're not going to – not yet. You're going to make me finish first. Understood?"

I nod. God, just a bit more of his touching and I-

He stops, the sexy fucker knowing just how to bring me to the edge.

"Now, take me inside you."

I reach down and take his cock in my hand, holding Maksim's cock straight as I lower myself down, down, and....

"Oh... *fuck*."

He glides into me with total ease, the words pouring from my mouth as I impale myself on him. Soon he's fully buried inside, all the way to the root. Maksim reaches around and grabs my ass, squeezing it hard and pushing me forward, urging me to grind on him.

I move back and forth, rocking my hips, his eyes tracing over every bit of my body. I love the way he looks at me, love the way he touches me, love the way he feels deep, so deep, inside.

But in the middle of it all, I remember his order – I have to make him come before I'm allowed to. His growls, the way he sensually narrows his eyes, tells me he's close.

"Are you ready?" he asks. "Ready to feel me explode inside of you?"

"Yes. Please. I'm so ready." My own orgasm is so close I'm right on the verge of disobeying his command.

But mercifully, Maksim grunts hard, and I know he's there. He thrusts up into me, holding me in place as his cock erupts. He releases into me, and I can't hold back even if I want to. My back arches and the climax flows through me with total, blissful warmth. It's like nothing else I've ever felt before.

I feel Maksim's seed drip down, tickling my inner thigh. He moves his hands slowly up and down my sides, touching me in a totally loving manner that serves as a sharp contrast to how aggressive he'd been only a few moments before.

He rises, lifting me off him and holding me as if I weigh nothing at all. He places me on my feet on the soft, plush rug as if I'm made of China. Then he wraps his arm around me, kissing my shoulder and holding me tightly.

I allow myself a small smile. Maksim knows how to take care of me during lovemaking and knows how to take care of me after. He leads us to the sofa and lays on his back where I place my head on his chest, totally blissed out as he pulls a blanket over us.

There's a warmth, a rightness to being this close to him, a man I'm still getting the measure of. Weird, considering I've never felt this plugged in with anyone before.

As I lay there, content, real life slaps me in the face. I realize I have a life outside this bubble. A messy, complicated life that involves a business I'm supposed to be running.

It's like getting a splash of cold water to the face.

With a sigh that feels like I'm setting down something precious, I wiggle out from under Maksim's arm and start collecting my clothes, each piece a step back to reality.

Maksim stirs, his voice sleepy but laced with a hint of concern. "Where are you going?"

I pause, half-dressed, and shoot him a look. "I have a life and a job that doesn't involve getting kidnapped or debating with mobsters."

He props himself up on one elbow, that familiar smirk playing on his lips. "You sure? Because that sounds like a full-time job to me."

I roll my eyes, even as a reluctant smile tugs at my lips. "Ha-ha, very funny. Someone's got to keep the city's dogs happy, and last I checked, that's me."

Slipping on the last of my clothes, I turn back to him, caught between the pull of this newfound connection and the call of my own world. "Listen," I start, trying to sound more confident than I feel, "this...whatever this is, it's new territory for me. But I've got a business to run and a life to sort out."

He watches me, amusement and something deeper in his gaze. "I know," he says, the weight of his words carrying a promise. "Just remember, you've got my number. For anything." Maksim snatches a look at his watch, eyeing the time with a hint of something that might be responsibility. "Looks like I need to get moving too," he announces, standing up and letting the blanket cascade away with a carelessness that speaks volumes about his comfort in his own skin.

And there he is, in all his glory, not a stitch on him, and completely unbothered by it. Me? I'm momentarily rooted to the spot, my exit strategy suddenly looking less appealing. The view's enough to short-circuit any sensible thought, leaving me wondering if a speedy departure is really in my best interests.

Maksim's gaze dances over my own body, his eyes lingering. I love the way he looks at me.

"As much as I appreciate the view from here, we really should get a move on," he chuckles, pulling on some clothes on with a speed that suggests he's no stranger to quick changes.

Following him through the house, I'm hit once again by the sheer size and grandeur of it. It's like stepping into a different world, one where every corner and corridor speaks of a life miles away from my own.

He catches me looking around, an eyebrow raised in silent question. "What's on your mind?" he asks, that playful edge still present in his voice.

"Oh, just calculating how many Murphy beds I could fit in this place," I reply, throwing him a smirk. "Turns out, it's a lot."

Maksim laughs, a sound that's becoming increasingly familiar and welcome. "Well, if you ever need more space, feel free to expand into here. I'm sure we could find a corner for a dog or two."

Just as we're about to leave, a car rolls up, cutting through the late morning calm like a scene straight out of a suburban fantasy. Behind the wheel is an older woman, her demeanor speaking volumes of warmth and authority, and in the back seat, a young girl who could easily win a cuteness contest.

Maksim's face lights up with both pride and affection, a sight that's oddly disarming.

The door swings open, and the girl pops out of her booster seat and onto the driveway, curiosity written all over her face. "Who's the lady?"

Maksim smiles at her and introduces me. "She's a friend."

But little Miss Adelina, with a name as charming as her curious little self, isn't about to let that vague introduction slide. "Friend? Is she your new best friend?" Adelina's eyes are wide, her questions fired off with the rapid precision of a seasoned interrogator.

Maksim chuckles, a sound both warm and a tad evasive. "A very special friend, Ade."

She's not satisfied, her gaze flitting between us like she's putting together a puzzle. "Do you have a dog? What's your favorite color? Will you come to my ballet recital?" The questions tumble out, each one more adorable and probing than the last.

I squat down in front of her, putting my hands on my knees. She's so adorable it hurts – and she looks just like her father.

"Do I have a dog? Little lady, you asked the right person that question – I don't have just one dog, I have *dogs*, with an S."

"Really? How many? What kind of dogs? How big are they?"

Maksim gently cuts in, "Ade, let's not overwhelm my friend, okay?"

Adelina huffs, a miniature version of a grown-up sigh. "Okay, but I still wanna know if she'll come to the recital."

With a laugh that's both apologetic and filled with paternal love, Maksim scoops her up. "You're being a bit too forward, young lady," he tells her, but it's clear there's no real reprimand there, just a father's amusement at his daughter's inquisitive nature.

Standing there, watching them, I'm struck by the duality of Maksim Morozov. Here he is, a man whose life is shrouded in danger and shadows, displaying such undeniable love and tenderness for his daughter. It's a juxtaposition that's both baffling and intriguing, painting him in shades I'm only just beginning to understand.

How does he reconcile these two worlds? The loving father and the feared mobster? It's a puzzle, a complex enigma wrapped in the guise of a man who's just introduced me as a friend to his daughter.

Adelina's eyes meet mine, bright with curiosity and something akin to approval. Before anyone can say anything else, the woman steps out of the car.

"Come along, Ade," she says, her tone firm. "Let's leave your father be while he speaks to his *friend*."

The strange emphasis she puts on the final word, along with her quick up-and-down of me with her eyes, makes it clear she understands I'm not at the house for business.

"Thank you, Irina," Maksim says as the pair vanish into the house.

Maksim, with his unexpected depths and contradictions, has firmly caught my interest. Figuring him out, understanding the man behind the mystery, suddenly feels like a challenge I'm more than willing to accept.

CHAPTER 18

Riding shotgun in Maksim's sleek car, I'm hit with this wave of rightness. It's bizarre, considering the whirlwind of events that's been my life since he waltzed into it, but here I am, feeling downright cozy next to the most mysterious man I've ever met.

Pulling up in front of the shop, Maksim breaks the comfortable silence.

"We're still on for Friday, right?"

His voice holds a hint of something I can't quite pin down—hope, maybe? It's funny, considering the chaos that's become my new normal since he showed up, that he's worried about a date.

"Yes, we are," I affirm, surprised by my own eagerness. It feels like ages since he asked, even though it's barely been a day.

Before I can process, Maksim's out of the car, moving with effortless grace to open my door. Gentlemanly moves from a man with a not-so-gentle reputation.

His goodbye kiss lands softly on my cheek, a chaste contrast to the fiery connection we've been tiptoeing around. "See you Friday," he says, a promise in his voice that sends a thrill through me.

He ushers me toward the shop with a hand on my back, a fleeting touch that somehow says more than words could. Then, he's off, striding back to his car, leaving me to stare after him, a bundle of contradictions in a well-tailored suit.

Stepping into the shop, I can't shake the feeling I'm walking a tightrope between my old life and something entirely new, thrilling, and utterly terrifying. Maksim, with his unexpected chivalry and his even more unexpected kisses, has thrown my world into a beautiful chaos.

I dart inside, but not before throwing a saucy glance back at Maksim. Something about him, all boss-man behind the wheel of that luxury ride, sends a sizzle straight through me, makes my pussy clench. It's ridiculous, really, how much that sight cranks my engine.

But the chaos inside the shop pulls me back into reality. Ty's in the thick of it, surrounded by a canine tornado that's one tail wag short of a disaster. I burst out laughing as I dive into the fray beside him.

"Sorry I'm late to the party!" I exclaim, half out of breath and totally amused by the pandemonium.

Ty shoots me a grin, wrestling with a particularly enthusiastic pup. "Trust me, it's more bark than bite around here. Just another day at the office!" he quips, clearly unfazed by the furry whirlwind around us.

Helping Ty wrangle the dogs back into some semblance of order, I'm struck by the absurdity and utter joy of my day-to-day. From being kidnapped by mobsters to herding excitable dogs, my life's nothing if not varied.

As the last dog settles down, Ty and I share a look of camaraderie and shared insanity that comes from doing what we do.

"You owe me a coffee for this one, boss," Ty jokes, dusting off his hands with a theatrical sigh.

I laugh, already plotting to bring him his favorite fancy latte as a peace offering. "Deal. But you're telling me all the gossip I missed," I shoot back, ready to dive into the day's work with renewed vigor.

"Speaking of gossip…" He glances toward the front of the shop, toward the street where Maksim had been parked only a short time ago.

"Later, later…"

The moment the last yappy chorus quiets down, I'm on damage control, picking up after our furry guests. There's a certain art to navigating through the aftermath of a doggie daycare day, a blend of grace and a lot of elbow grease. But hey, someone's got to do it.

Next on the agenda is some quality yard time for a couple of our regulars: a hyperactive Beagle named Buster, and Luna, a Husky with a penchant for dramatic howls that could give opera singers a run for their money. As I let them out into the yard, the familiar sights and sounds of my neighborhood wrap around me like a well-worn jacket. It's comforting, grounding, and just a tiny bit suffocating all at once.

Leaning against the fence, watching Buster's relentless pursuit of his own tail and Luna's more contemplative stalking of a particularly interesting blade of grass, I find my mind wandering. Maksim Morozov. The man's a total mystery, with a dash of undeniable allure. And I am caught up in his orbit, contemplating a date with a man who's as dangerous as he is captivating.

Let's be real for a moment—my body's already made up its mind about him. The man's touched me in ways I didn't even know I wanted to be touched. And the scary part? I know he's just getting started. The thought alone is enough to send shivers down my spine. What else is he capable of if he's already left such an unforgettable impression?

But it's not just the physical pull that's got me all tangled up. He's a father—a good one, from the little glimpse I've had. Watching him with Adelina stirred something in me, a mix of admiration and curiosity. What's their story? What happened to Adelina's mother? These are the pieces of the puzzle I find myself eager to solve, questions I hope to explore on our date. Because, oh yes, there's going to be a date.

As Buster finally catches his tail, only to look bewildered at his own success, and Luna lets out a satisfied sigh, settling down in the shade, I make my decision. I'm going on that date with Maksim. Because, frankly, the man's sparked a curiosity in me that I can't ignore. And who knows? Maybe, just maybe, he'll surprise me.

Breezing back into the shop, adrenaline still pumping from my reflections outside, I dive straight into the day's work alongside Ty. But first—those cameras. With a purposeful stride, I find and snag the recorder and the camera, flicking them off with a satisfaction that's as sharp as it is swift.

Holding them, I cast a glance toward the Murphy bed, a flush creeping up my neck as I recall the private show Maksim had front-row seats to. The realization that he was watching is bizarrely exhilarating, adding an edge to the memory that sends a thrill through me.

The rest of the day blurs into a canine ballet, with Ty and me as the conductors, until the final wagging tail exits stage left. That's when Ty launches his inquisition.

"Okay, spill. Who gave you that shiner?" he asks, his eyes narrowed.

Deep breath. It's time for the truth, minus a few choice details.

"Alright, deep dive into Tory's soap opera," I start, leaning against the counter for dramatic effect. "So, Ned left me a lovely parting gift—a loan from the mob."

Ty's eyebrows shoot up, but I plow on, the words tumbling out now.

"Enter Maksim, claiming I need to pay up. There's been some...flirting," I admit, a half-grin sneaking through despite the seriousness of my situation. "Maksim has cleared the debt, but I don't know if everything is okay."

Ty's reaction is a masterpiece of shock and disbelief, his mouth agape as he processes each revelation. "Holy shit, Tory. This is...a lot."

"Yeah, tell me about it," I agree, leaning back with a sigh. The bit about the camera, though? That's a detail I choose to keep to myself, especially since it's already been dealt with—destroyed, to be exact.

Ty shakes his head, awe and concern etched across his face. "Just when I thought running a dog daycare was as exciting as it gets. You okay, though?"

I nod, a determined set to my jaw. "Yeah, I am. Thanks to Maksim, weirdly enough. Friday's still a go, and I intend to find out just how deep this rabbit hole goes."

As we finish locking up, Ty shakes his head, amusement and disbelief mingling in his expression. "Your life's turned into a full-blown action movie, Tory. You realize that, right? Going on a date with Maksim is just... Are you sure you're not a bit out of your mind?"

I can't help but laugh, leaning back against the closed door. "Maybe just a tad. But, Ty, I think it's going to be alright. I actually trust him," I confess, surprising myself a little with the conviction in my voice.

Ty gives me a look, one that's part skepticism, part genuine concern. "Good luck, then. I really hope it works out for you. But let's not forget how well your last rendezvous with a bad boy went," he says, reminding me of Ned's introduction into my life—charm dialed up to a hundred and trouble written all over him.

"Yeah, yeah, I know," I admit, rolling my eyes. "You tried to warn me off him, remember? But the more you talked, the more appealing Ned became. It's like you were his hype man."

Ty laughs at that, a hearty, genuine sound. "True, I might have accidentally sold you on the dearly departed Ned. But you've always had a soft spot for the bad types."

He's not wrong, and I'm not about to deny it. "Guilty as charged," I say with a grin. "But Maksim's different. He's not Ned."

"Sure, he's different," Ty concedes, his tone dripping with sarcasm. "He's a criminal with a nicer car and a bit of distinguished gray. Totally different league."

I chuckle, despite the niggling doubts his words stir up. "Come on. Maksim's got layers. He's complicated."

Ty's laughter fades, replaced by a look of earnest worry. "Tor, I just don't want you to get hurt. Ned was a disaster, and Maksim... well, he's still a wild card. Just promise me you'll be careful, okay?"

I nod, feeling a warmth for my friend's unease. "I will. I promise. My heart's telling me this is right. But," I glance away, contemplating the turmoil of my emotions, "I guess there's a part of me, and definitely you, questioning this whole thing."

As we say our goodbyes and I head for my office slash bedroom, the weight of our conversation lingers. Ty's words echo in my mind. My heart's all in, betting on this connection with Maksim, on the flicker of something real between us. But my head, and Ty, well, they're not so easily convinced.

Flopping into my office chair, I can't shake the feeling of being at a crossroads. Choosing Maksim, stepping further into his world—is a gamble my heart's willing to make.

CHAPTER 19

MAKSIM

One month later...

A rare grin spreads across my face as I glance at my phone. I'd arranged for a bouquet of flowers to be delivered to Tory, a gesture to show her she's on my mind. The confirmation comes in the form of a photo she sends me—her, radiating happiness, clutching the flowers, with one of her dogs making a comedic attempt at a floral snack.

Our first outing that Friday set the tone for what was to come. I'd taken her to Nightscape, an exclusive spot where the outside world fades away, leaving only the connection between those within its walls.

The night was a blend of shared stories, laughter that filled the air, and a mutual discovery that drew us closer. As the evening wound down, the connection we'd nurtured found its expression in more private ways.

Since that night, our paths haven't crossed daily, yet not a day goes by without us talking, sharing pieces of our days, our thoughts. It's a rhythm we've fallen into naturally, conversations that span from the mundane to the profound, interspersed with moments spent together that only deepen the bond we're building.

Each time we meet, it's as if we're picking up right where we left off, a seamless continuation of the exploration we began the first night. There's a comfort in her presence, a sense of rightness that comes from being with someone who understands me, challenges me, and accepts me—all at once.

This connection is something I hadn't anticipated, yet here I am, drawn to her in ways I'm still unraveling. And as I set my phone down, ready to focus on the tasks awaiting my attention, a part of me is already looking forward to our next conversation, our next meeting.

My train of thought is suddenly derailed by Adelina's booming announcement, "Uncle Aleksey's here!" Her energy could power the city, and despite the near damage to my eardrums, I can't help but grin. "Thanks for the heads-up, princess," I manage amidst her giggles when I rub my ear.

The moment is light, full of laughter, until Aleksey strides in, and Adelina, ever the curious one, launches the question I wasn't prepared to field just yet.

"When is your girlfriend gonna come over again?" The innocence of her query does nothing to ease the tension that snaps tight in the room.

My wince is automatic, a reflex to the unexpected complication her words bring, especially with Aleksey now fully tuned in, a wry glint in his eye as he saunters over to my bar.

Aleksey's amusement is as clear as day, his intrigue palpable as he helps himself to a drink without invitation. The situation's delicacy isn't lost on me; Adelina's simple question suddenly feels like a loaded gun.

Turning to Adelina, I muster as much nonchalance as I can. "We'll see honey. Life is busy right now." It's an attempt to deflect, to buy time in a conversation I'm not ready to have, especially not with Aleksey's attentive ears.

Aleksey's chuckle from the bar sends a clear message—he's found a new angle in our ever-evolving game of chess. "A girlfriend, Maksim? That's a new twist," he teases, sipping his drink with an air of casual provocation.

I meet his gaze, unflinching, the alpha in me rising to the surface. "Life's full of surprises, Aleksey. Just like our business," I retort, the undercurrent of my words suggesting the depth of complexities he well knows.

The room's charged with an unspoken understanding, a recognition of the delicate balance between personal lives and the demands of our Bratva existence. Adelina, oblivious to the tension, simply smiles, satisfied with her role in the day's drama.

"No way your mean old dad has a girlfriend, little Ade," Aleksey jests, a playful challenge in his tone.

Adelina, undeterred and full of youthful confidence, fires back, "He does too! Her name is Tory. She's got pretty red hair and she has lots and lots of doggies."

The room shifts palpably at her declaration, the air thickening as Aleksey's amusement turns to a glare directed at me.

Catching the change in mood, Adelina decides it's her cue to exit. "I'm gonna go find Irina. I'm hungry," she announces, a strategic retreat from the grown-ups' conversation. I send her off with a blown kiss, pride swelling in me as she skips out of the room.

Once she's gone, Aleksey turns his full attention to me, the previous levity gone. "You're dating that woman?" His voice is sharp, cutting through any pretense of jest.

I meet his gaze squarely, the weight of my position and my personal life colliding in this moment. "Yes, I am," I confirm, my voice steady. "Tory's not just 'that woman.' She's important to me."

Aleksey's eyes narrow, assessing, perhaps trying to find a crack in my resolve. The silence stretches, thick with unspoken challenges and the weight of my declaration.

Amidst the tension, Aleksey's penchant for provocation rears its head. "Important, huh? What's next, Maksim? You going to make our little dog watcher a respectable wife?" His tone is laced with mockery, the kind that ignites a fierce protectiveness in me.

That urge, primal and fierce, to leap across the desk and wipe the smug look off his face for even insinuating Tory could be anything less than respected, surges within me. Yet I maintain the facade of calm I've honed over the years, my expression meticulously neutral despite the tumult inside.

"Careful, brother," I warn, my voice low, the threat implicit. "Your insinuations are not appreciated. Not when it comes to her." My stance is clear, unyielding. Tory is off-limits.

"Why are you thinking with your dick instead of your brain?" Aleksey pushes, skepticism and accusation weaving through his tone like a sharp needle. He doesn't pause for breath, plunging straight into a lecture on my apparent misstep. "Clearing her debt—what were you thinking? It's not just a lapse in judgment."

He leans in, his words a calculated jab. "Our father was not pleased, Maksim. And he'll be even less thrilled when he finds out how serious things have become between you and this woman. You're getting too close. A fling is one thing, but bringing her near your family, *our* family..."

The air between us crackles with tension, his challenge laid bare. But my response is measured, a counterpoint to his provocation. "My decisions are mine to make. Tory's not a mistake. And our relationship is not up for discussion."

His smirk is undiminished, but there's a flicker of something else in his eyes—recognition, maybe, or the acknowledgment of a line he's treading too closely.

I go on, meeting his challenge directly, my voice calm but laced with an unmistakable edge. "My decisions—how I handle my obligations and my personal life—are not up for debate. Clearing Tory's debt was a decision made with full awareness of the consequences."

The tension between us is palpable. "And as for our father," I continue, "I am well prepared to face any repercussions. My priorities are clear."

Aleksey, with a smirk that could provoke a saint, leans back and delivers his jab. "So, the mighty Maksim has finally been tamed by a pair of perky tits and red hair? What's next? Trading in your guns for bouquets?" His tone drips with mockery, a challenge wrapped in humor, aimed directly at my resolve.

"Enough," I cut in, my voice brooking no argument. "The debt is settled. Tory's name is cleared from our books. We're done here."

Aleksey tries to jump back in, his words sharpened with the intent to twist the narrative his way. "But Maksim—"

"I said, it's over," I snap, the edge in my voice like a blade. The finality I inject into those words aims to sever this conversation.

The room falls silent, tension humming in the air like a charged storm. Aleksey pauses, his jaw clenching as he processes my stance. Then, with a scoff that's both a dismissal and a challenge, he rises from his seat.

Without a glance back, without the barest nod of departure, he strides out of the room, the heavy silence his only companion. The door clicks shut behind him, the sound a definitive end to our heated exchange.

As the door closes behind him, a sense of resolve settles over me. This confrontation was inevitable, a clash of principles and priorities. But standing my ground, defending my choices and the life I'm choosing to lead with Tory, it's a statement—a declaration that some lines are not to be crossed, not even by family.

CHAPTER 20

TORY

I check the clock, noting the dwindling time before my appointment, and then glance over the room at the calm pack of dogs. Ty's engrossed in his phone, giving occasional pats to a bulldog that's all but snoring.

"Ty," I call out, snagging my bag and keys off the counter, "I'm about to head out. Listen, I'm thinking of giving you a whole day off to make up for today. You've been a rockstar, especially with Nicky's spot still open."

Nicky never returned after the day I was kidnapped. No call, nothing. So we've been a bit shorthanded.

He looks up, a wide grin breaking across his face. "A whole day off? What, you trying to get rid of me or something, Tor?"

I can't help but roll my eyes, a laugh threatening to break free. "Yes, that's exactly it. I can hardly stand the sight of you. No, but for real, you've been incredible the past few weeks. It's been a madhouse around here."

He laughs, standing up to stretch his limbs. "Don't worry about it. Honestly, this is the best job I've ever had. Beats sitting at a desk any day and I get to work with my bestie."

I smile, feeling genuinely grateful for his easy-going nature and the seamless way we work together. "Alright, but the offer stands. You deserve a break, even if these guys," I gesture at the lounging dogs, "are being unusually angelic today."

"Deal," he says with a nod. "But I'm holding you to finding someone less charming than me. Good luck with that."

"I'll do my best," I chuckle, heading toward the door. "Seriously, though, take a day. You've more than earned it."

As I'm almost out the door, Ty's curiosity gets the better of him. "Hey, where you headed in such a rush?" he calls out, then immediately winces. "Sorry, that's me being nosy again."

I pause, turning back with a smirk. "No worries, I'm just off to the doctor. Nothing serious, just some stubborn bug that's been hanging around too long. Got me feeling all sorts of worn out and a bit queasy."

His concern is immediate, a frown creasing his brow. "Ah, that sounds rough. Make sure the doc gives you the meds you need. We can't have you down for the count. I can't take a day off if you're sick," he teases.

I laugh. "Your concern is duly noted. I'll catch you later."

Stepping out into the brilliant embrace of an April day, a grin spreads across my face. The sun's shining and here I am, strutting down the street like I own it, on my way to the doctor. But my mind's not really on my health. Nope, it's hijacked by thoughts of Maksim—Mr. Tall, Dark, and Dangerously Handsome in his suits... and, well, decidedly less dressed.

I'm replaying every moment, from the way his hands map out territories on my skin to that deep, rumble of a voice he reserves for our most intimate occasions. It's enough to make a girl forget she's actually walking in the real world, which I do, spectacularly, almost becoming roadkill in my little fantasy land.

Ten minutes later, I'm at the doctor, pen in hand, breezing through the paperwork like it's nothing—until I hit the question about possibly being pregnant. Talk about a record scratch moment. My eyes about pop out of my head as it hits me—Maksim and I have been all about the passion and totally not about protection. And birth control? Haven't thought about that since the Ned era ended. No action, no need, right?

Shit.

With a gulp that feels like swallowing a tennis ball, I tick 'yes' on the question.

Next thing I know, I'm shuffling into the exam room, pee cup in hand, feeling like I'm about to audition for the lead role in a drama I did not sign up for. They tell me to leave it in the designated spot, which suddenly feels like dropping off a bomb, not a pee sample.

I'm perched on the exam table, swaddled in this oh-so-flattering paper gown, trying not to look as frazzled as I feel. And all I can do is wait, wondering how a quick visit to the doc escalated into a potential life-altering moment.

The moment my doctor waltzes in with that telltale smile, my heart does a weird somersault. Boom, just like that, she drops the P-bomb. "Congratulations, you're pregnant!"

My face must be a masterpiece of shock and awe, because she instantly shifts into damage control mode.

"You okay?" she asks.

"Oh, I'm fine, really," I manage to sputter out, my voice sounding like it's coming from someone else. *Fine?* My brain's doing cartwheels, my heart's racing for the Olympics, and I'm sitting here in a paper gown feeling anything but fine. "I just, I wasn't even thinking about, well, *anything* I guess. Holy shit. Sorry, Doc."

"No need to apologize. So this wasn't a planned pregnancy, I'm guessing."

I shake my head and a near-hysterical laugh escaping me. "Um, no. Not even close."

She nods. "Do you want to discuss your options?"

My answer flies out before my brain even catches up. "My options? I'm keeping my baby."

Just like that. I've barely known I'm pregnant long enough to process it, and here I am, all in, ready to embark on this wild ride of motherhood.

She gives me a soft, "I see," coupled with a nod that's got more empathy in it than I've seen in a long while. "Judging by the date of your last period and your HCG levels, you're about four weeks along," she explains.

She instructs me to set up an appointment with my OB/GYN for a full exam the next week, including ultrasound. She hands over a starter kit of prenatal vitamins like I've just won some sort of bizarre lottery and piles on the reading material.

"Congratulations, Tory. Take care of yourself," she says, leaving me to get dressed and step back into my life, which has just taken the most unexpected turn.

Walking out of the doctor's office, the world seems to shift beneath my feet. It's like stepping onto a movie set where I'm the lead in a plot twist I didn't see coming. Craving a moment of solitude, I veer into a nearby coffee shop, my mind a whirlwind of thoughts and emotions.

Queuing up for my usual caffeine fix, I halt mid-order. Right, no caffeine when you're playing host to a tiny human. It's a trivial change, but it slams home the reality of my new situation. Opting for a decaf, I find a quiet corner to process the bombshell that's just been dropped into my lap.

The reality of my circumstances starts to really sink in. The father of my child isn't just any guy; he's a Russian mob enforcer/boss-in-training. Our whirlwind romance has been thrilling, sure, but it's also placed me smack dab in the middle of a world I know is fraught with danger. Can he, will he, be able to keep that life away from me...from my child?

And let's not gloss over the fact we've only been dating a month and I got pregnant the very first time we were together. If that's not a story line straight out of a daytime drama, I don't know what is.

This secret, this tiny, life-altering secret, is mine to carry for now. As I sip on my decidedly less-than-thrilling decaf, I can't help but wonder about the future. Maksim and I are in uncharted waters, a place where passion meets reality with a side order of mafia complications.

Keeping this under wraps feels like the only move, at least until I can get my head around it all. The thought of bringing a child into the mix? That's a conversation for another day—a day when I've had more than a few minutes to come to terms with becoming a mom.

CHAPTER 21

MAKSIM

The moment I kill the engine of my car, parked in front of my father's mansion, anger courses through me. The thought of having to postpone my evening plans with Tory for some asinine family meeting boils my blood.

It's Aleksey's doing—I'm sure of it. He must've run to our father, spinning tales about our recent confrontation. The notion that I'm being dragged into a parental arbitration at my age is both infuriating and demeaning. As I storm toward the house, the gravity of the situation sits heavily on my shoulders.

Stepping inside, the tension momentarily lifts at the sight of Irina and Adelina, my world, seated at the sprawling dining room table, engrossed in a puzzle. Adelina's eyes light up as she spots me.

"Papa! Come help us with the puzzle," she calls out, her voice a mix of excitement and command that only an eight-year-old can muster.

I smile, despite the storm brewing inside me. "Not right now, precious," I respond, my tone softening. "I need to talk to *Dedushka*. It's important."

Her face falls for a moment, disappointment fleeting across her features before she nods, understanding more than a child her age should. "Okay, Papa. But come back soon, okay? We need help."

I lean down, pressing a kiss to her forehead, the anger momentarily subsided by her presence. "I promise, Princess. I'll be back before you even notice I'm gone."

As I turn to leave, Adelina's small hand catches mine, her touch gentle yet firm. "Papa, why do you look so upset?" she inquires, her innocence piercing through my carefully maintained facade. Internally, I chastise myself for letting my emotions become so visible, especially around her.

Irina's observant gaze lands on us, a silent witness to this exchange. I should've been more cautious, more controlled.

"Is it because of Uncle Aleksey?" Adelina's question draws me back, her intuition surprising me.

I kneel down to her level, masking my emotions with a practiced ease. "What makes you say that, Princess?" I probe gently.

She shrugs, a small frown marring her brow. "He didn't even stop to say hi to me or Irina."

Her observation hits close to home, highlighting the tension that's been brewing, yet I find myself defending Aleksey, despite my own frustrations. "Uncle Aleksey probably has a lot on his mind, Princess. Important adult stuff, you understand?" I offer her a reassuring smile. "I'm sure he'll make it up to you and say hello before he leaves."

Adelina seems to ponder this for a moment before nodding, accepting my explanation with the trusting innocence only a child could have.

With a final squeeze of Adelina's hand, I promise myself to shield her from these family storms, to keep the innocence in her eyes untainted by my world.

Striding up the grand staircase, a wave of frustration washes over me for letting Adelina see the cracks in my armor. She's too clever for her own good, and it's only a matter of time before she starts connecting the dots about what I do. A silent vow forms in my mind—I'll protect her from it all for as long as I can.

My phone vibrates, a brief distraction from my thoughts. It's Tory. Her text reads, *Guess our wild night's canceled? Shame, was looking forward to seeing you try to outdo last time.*

I can't help but smirk, typing back quickly, *Wild night's just delayed, not canceled. I promise, worth the wait.*

Her reply comes with a playful edge, *I'll be the judge of that. Here's something to ensure you don't forget me,* followed by a picture that ramps up my anticipation—a bold, teasing glimpse of Tory that sends my pulse racing.

In the photo she's dressed in nothing but a pair of light blue panties, her arm crossing her breasts just enough to cover her nipples. She's smiling, her red hair tossed about her face. The picture is hot as hell; I pause for a moment to compose myself, my cock stiffening to attention.

I'm looking forward to ripping those panties off, I reply.

Another picture follows, this one with her thumb hooked under the waistband of said panties, teasing me by pulling on the waistband but not enough to give me a glimpse. I growl like an animal as I take in the sight.

Using all the restraint I have, I slip my phone back into my pocket and continue.

First work, then play.

The exchange, brief as it is, sharpens my focus. My eyes lock onto the door of the study, and I'm ready.

Mulling over everything as I approach my father's study, a decision crystallizes in my mind—Tory and Adelina need to get to know one another better. The thought alone sets my pulse hammering, a heady brew of anticipation and anxiety that dwarfs any apprehension about the impending family showdown.

Pushing the door open, I find myself walking straight into the heart of tension, the air thick with silent confrontations yet to unfold. My father greets me with a nod, his face a reflection of my own feelings about this forced gathering— irritation masked by a veneer of necessary family diplomacy.

Then there's Aleksey. He doesn't waste a moment, immediately taking the offensive, his disdain barely concealed. I attempt a greeting, a gesture of peace, but he's dismissive, treating my effort as if it's beneath him.

"Good of you to finally show up," Aleksey sneers, his words dripping with a venom that's all too familiar. Clearly, he's enjoying this, the opportunity to cast me as the wayward brother, the one stepping out of line.

My jaw clenches at his tone, every instinct urging me to hit back, to wipe that smug look off his face. But I hold back, aware that any outburst plays right into his hands. Father's watching us both, a silent arbiter of our sibling rivalry turned cold war.

"So, Aleksey, what's the urgent matter that couldn't wait?" I ask, forcing neutrality into my voice, even as I brace myself for his onslaught of accusations or demands.

He turns to our father. "Maksim's lost it, thinking with his dick instead of his brain," he spits out.

His words, meant to provoke, barely register. I brush off the jab. "Aleksey," I start, my voice low, controlled, "you brought our business into my home, risked exposing Adelina to it." The memory alone fuels my anger, but I'm keeping a tight lid on it, for now.

Aleksey, smug fuck as always, fires back, "Using your daughter as a shield now? That's low, even for you." He crosses the final line, suggesting Tory's nothing more than a transaction to me. "Is that piece of ass really good enough to pay a hundred grand for?"

That's it. Any semblance of control snaps. I'm across the room before I know it, my fist connecting with Aleksey's face in a satisfying thud. He reels, then comes back at me, his punch catching my jaw.

Father's shouting, trying to intervene, but it's white noise. All I see is Aleksey, all I feel is this raw, primal need to protect what's mine—Tory's honor, Adelina's innocence.

The room suddenly fills with the bulk of our father's enforcers, their hands gripping us firmly, yanking my brother and me apart. I barely register the pain from the blow Aleksey landed; my focus is on the blood streaming from his nose—a small victory in a battle that shouldn't have been fought.

"Enough!" Father's voice cuts through the tension like a knife. "Never again, Maksim," he barks, his gaze drilling into me. "We stand together. Always." It's a reminder, a command, that our family's unity is paramount, no matter the personal grievances.

His eyes then shift to Aleksey, hard and unyielding. "And you, remember this—Maksim is your elder brother. His path is set. Yours is to support, not undermine." It's a declaration, laying bare the hierarchy within our family.

As the guards release their hold, I straighten, brushing off my suit, the taste of blood in my mouth a bitter reminder of the line I'd crossed.

"Enough of this bullshit," Aleksey sneers as he grabs his coat. "I came here for a discussion, and now I'm being put in my place as the spare." He strides toward the office door. "Enjoy your temporary seat at the table, brother, when you finally get it. We'll see how long it takes before you're begging me to take over." Aleksey makes his dramatic exit, the door slamming shut with a finality that seems to echo through the silent room.

The urge to chase after him, to confront the storm of accusations and threats head-on, surges within me. It's only the memory of my father's stern command, his reminder of the

THE ARRANGEMENT | 149

fragile balance we're forced to navigate in this family drama, that holds me back.

I turn to face Father, the frustration and anger clear in my expression. "How am I supposed to just stand by and let him—"

"Enough, Maksim," Father cuts in, his voice firm yet weary. "Chasing after Aleksey will only escalate the problem. You need to be smart, not reactive."

I exhale slowly, trying to rein in the tumultuous mix of emotions Aleksey's words have stirred. "He's threatening everything we've built. Everything *you've* built with his adolescent temper tantrums," I argue.

Father sighs, then tosses me a handkerchief. I press it against my mouth, feeling the sting of Aleksey's blows, but it's his words, his blatant challenge to my future leadership, that left a deeper mark.

"So, this woman," Father begins, breaking the silence that had settled between us, "what's the story there?"

I meet his gaze, choosing my words with care. "I'm seeing her. It's serious." It feels like a confession, laying bare a part of my life I've kept shielded from the family dynamics. "She's going to be spending time with Adelina this weekend."

My father nods, a hint of a smile breaking through his usually stoic demeanor. "Good, good. It's about time you found someone." But then his expression sobers, the father in him giving way to the patriarch. "Just remember, Maksim, the family comes first. Always."

The words hang heavy between us. I understand the weight of his reminder, the duty that comes with my name, my blood. But the implication that Tory might somehow be a distraction, or worse, a liability, sits uneasily with me.

I nod, the gesture more automatic than agreeable. "I know where my loyalties lie." The words are firm, but internally, I'm wrestling with the notion that my personal happiness could ever be at odds with my obligations to the Bratva.

Father leans back in his chair, his gaze locking onto mine with an authority that's gone unchallenged for decades. "I'll talk to Aleksey," he states. "Make sure he understands—our business, it stays out of sight, especially from Adelina."

I find myself nodding, a silent thank you forming on my lips but never quite making it out. "Keeping that world away from her... it means everything."

He gives a curt nod, the matter settled in his mind, and in this moment, despite the tensions and the looming threats, I'm reminded of the lengths to which he'll go to protect the family.

"Remember, family first."

As I leave the room, the heaviness of Father's words settles over me. This "probation" is a reminder of the tightrope I walk—balancing my duties to the family with the desires of my heart. Tory has become a central figure in my life, her presence challenging the boundaries I've long adhered to.

Yet, despite the warnings, the constraints, I feel what I have with Tory is worth every risk, every potential fallout. I will protect it with everything I am.

CHAPTER 22

TORY

As I unzip my weekend bag, the thrill of staying with Maksim and finally getting to spend some real time with Adelina buzzes through me like a live wire. This weekend's not just about fun; it's a sneak peek into Maksim's world, a chance to see how he balances the dad life with... well, whatever else lurks in the shadows of his Bratva ties.

I start with the essentials, tossing in my favorite jeans and a couple of tees that walk the fine line between comfy and form fitting. I pause, my hand hovering over a drawer that's all daring and spice. "Why not?" I muse, pulling out a little black dress that screams trouble and a pair of heels that could kill a man—or at least make one follow me anywhere.

As I pack, my playlist is all upbeat vibes and bass drops, the kind of tunes that make you want to dance around in your underwear. But as I fold a slinky red top—perfect for a night in or a daring dash to the kitchen for midnight snacks— doubt creeps in. I'm getting all wound up for a weekend with a man who, for all his charm and undeniable sex appeal, is wrapped up in a world that could swallow me whole.

"Am I out of my mind?"

The excitement of spending time with Adelina, of being welcomed into their home, is tinged with this undercurrent of fear. What if this is it? The biggest mistake I've ever made, barreling toward me while I'm decked out in lace and optimism?

Shaking off the thought, I zip the bag closed. There's no turning back now, not when every beat of my heart is in sync with the rhythm of taking chances. I glance at the bag, my weekend of contradictions packed tight within, and let out a breath, thinking about my conversation with Ty earlier.

Walking back into the shop after the doc's revelation, Ty's there, eyebrows raised like he's ready to dissect every inch of my day.

"Spill it, girl. You look like you've seen a ghost... or a positive pregnancy test," he half-jokes, his knack for hitting too close to home making me wince.

The words just start spilling out of me in a torrent—I'm pregnant, caught up in this whirlwind romance with Maksim, and standing at the most bewildering crossroads of my life.

Ty's reaction is immediate and priceless. His eyes widen in shock, his mouth dropping open before it twists into this odd squint, a mix of congratulations and outright concern for my mental health. "You're what? *Pregnant?*" he finally manages, leaning forward as if the proximity might make the news less bombastic.

"Yeah," I reply, watching his expressions dance from surprise to something akin to delight, then back to skepticism. "With Maksim's baby. It's... a lot."

He blinks, then breaks into a grin that's both elated and a tad incredulous. "Holy *shit*, Tory! That's—wow, that's huge. But also, Maksim? Mr. Tall, Dark, and Bratva? You two have been busy, huh?"

I can't help but laugh, his blunt characterization of Maksim spot-on yet somehow endearing. "I guess we have. But seriously, I'm freaking out here. What am I supposed to do?"

Ty leans back, adopting a pose that's all mock solemnity, though his eyes are still twinkling with mischief. "Well, first off, congratulations are in order. And second, you're asking the wrong question. It's not what you're supposed to do; it's what you *want* to do."

I sigh, the reality of the situation settling back in. "I want... I don't know. I want this baby. And Maksim... there's something real there. But his life, his world—it's a lot to take on."

"What are you gonna do, Tor?" he asks, leaning on the counter like we're in some daytime drama. "Maksim's world is no fairy tale. It's like choosing to live in an action movie. With real bullets."

I sigh, running a hand through my hair. "I don't know. It's scary. His life, the dangers... Am I ready to be a part of that? To bring a baby into it?"

Ty lays it out straight. "You gotta tell him. This isn't just your story anymore—it's his too. And babe, you love him. That's worth fighting for, isn't it?"

His words hit, hard and true. Maksim, for all his alpha-ness, his complicated, dangerous life, he's become my heart's epicenter. But this—us plus a baby? I never saw it coming.

"Yeah," I finally answer, conviction stirring amidst the uncertainty. "Yeah, he needs to know. I just... how do you drop a bomb like that?"

"Just hit him with the truth," Ty advises, as if it's the simplest thing in the world. "It's generally a solid starting point."

I hesitate, my mind racing through every possible scenario. "But it's not just about the baby. I mean, how do I even begin to... wait, did you say that I *love* him?"

He cuts me off with a laugh that bounces off the shop walls, full of knowing and a bit too much amusement for my current state. "Girl, please. You're head over heels for him. It's like a neon sign flashing above your head every time his name comes up or he strides into this place. Stop fooling yourself."

I open my mouth, ready to protest, to deny it, but the words just hang there, suspended in a bubble of truth I've been avoiding. Love. It's a big word, a heavy concept, especially tangled up with a man whose life is a mosaic of complexity.

As I stand there, floundering in my own sea of denial, it hits me. Ty's right. Somewhere between the peril and the deep, intense moments with Maksim, I've fallen—hard. It's as terrifying as it is exhilarating.

"Shit, Ty, you're right. I do love him. He's just so different from anything I've known. He's tough but he's also soft with me. He's incredibly sexy, and the things he does to me..." I trail off.

Ty scoots closer, a conspiratorial grin on his face. "Do tell."

I laugh. "I never really thought that sex could be so *adventurous* before."

Ty leans forward, his expression thoughtful. "Sometimes lovers have this knack for unveiling parts of ourselves we never knew existed. If it's all good between you two, then why not explore? Just be safe and make sure you're both on the same page."

I grin at his supportive stance. "It's all good, really. Better than good."

His curiosity unabated, Ty waggles his eyebrows. "So, any juicy details you care to share with your bestie?"

I burst into laughter, shaking my head. "In your dreams. Some things are none of your business."

He chuckles, conceding with a playful roll of his eyes. "Alright, alright, keep your secrets. But just know, I'm here for you, Tory. No matter what."

A beat of silence passes.

"So, this weekend," I finally say, the words feeling both foreign and utterly right, "I'll tell him about the baby and, well, we'll see where it goes from there."

Ty nods, his expression softening to one of support. "His reaction will give you your answers. But for what it's worth,

I think you two have something special. And this baby just might be the best kind of surprise for you both."

"Thanks," I call over my shoulder, stepping out into the evening with a determination I didn't know I had. "Wish me luck."

"You won't need it," he calls back, his voice brimming with confidence. "Just tell him the truth."

The truth. It's simple, powerful, and utterly terrifying. But it's mine and Maksim's to face together, and I wouldn't have it any other way.

Snapping back to the present, the impending conversation with Maksim hits me like a ton of bricks. What if Maksim doesn't want this baby? He's already got Adelina, and I've no claim on him, no expectations for him to play the knight in shining armor.

As I place a pair of boots next to my saucy weekend selections, the fear of rejection gnaws at me. Maksim Morozov, with all his complexity and ties to a world far removed from my own, has no obligation to step into the role of father to this unexpected new life. The possibility of his rejection sends a shiver down my spine, the kind that leaves you feeling more isolated than ever before.

I take a deep breath, trying to steady my nerves. The bag looks back at me, a metaphorical Pandora's box of weekend wear and life-altering revelations. I've fallen for the man, truly and deeply, but this—this is a curve ball neither of us saw coming.

I have to be strong, for myself and for this baby. Maksim's reaction, whatever it may be, will chart the course of our future. It's a daunting prospect, stepping into the unknown, potentially facing it alone. But I resolve to face whatever comes with as much grace and strength as I can muster.

CHAPTER 23

TORY

Strolling through the Chicago Zoo, the sun's shining, and it feels like the perfect Saturday morning. Maksim, Adelina, and I are weaving through families and exhibits, and I've got to say, watching these two together is like peeking behind the curtain of Maksim's tough exterior.

"Okay, Papa," Adelina beams up at her dad, her energy absolutely infectious, "what's my favorite animal? Bet you can't guess!"

Maksim chuckles, ruffling her hair affectionately. "Penguins, isn't it? You've only told me about a hundred times."

Adelina nods, practically bouncing with excitement. "Yes! Can we go see them now, please?"

"We certainly can, Princess."

As we make our way to the penguin habitat, there's this warmth in Maksim's eyes that I haven't seen before. It's touching, really, seeing how he's completely wrapped around her little finger.

At the penguin exhibit, Adelina's practically glued to the glass, her laughter filling the air as the penguins dive and play. "Look at that one, Papa! He's doing flips!" she exclaims, pointing eagerly.

Maksim leans down, his voice low and warm. "He's showing off for you, I think."

This whole scene is like a snapshot of a life I'm only just starting to understand. With Irina off visiting her son for the weekend, it's just us, a little makeshift family navigating a day out. And it's nice. More than nice, actually.

"I wish Irina was here," Adelina muses aloud, glancing up at her papa.

He smiles at her gently as he explains. "She deserves a break. Plus, it gives us a chance to spend time together, just the three of us."

Adelina turns to me, her eyes gleaming with an idea. "Tory, if you were an animal, what would you be?"

I ponder for a moment, then play along with a smile. "Hmm, maybe a dolphin? They're smart, love to have fun, and they stick together."

Adelina claps her hands, delighted. "I like dolphins! You can be the dolphin, and I'll be the penguin. We can be zoo buddies!"

Laughing, I nod, fully on board with our new imaginary roles. "Zoo buddies for life," I agree.

Hanging out at the zoo, watching Maksim with Adelina, I'm hit with how much he shields her from his other world. And me? I'm diving headfirst into it, unsure but intrigued by the complexities of this man who can switch from Bratva boss to doting dad in a heartbeat.

As we wrap up our zoo adventure, I find myself caught between the laughter and the reality of stepping into their world. "You know, Maksim, today's been really something," I say, trying to capture the whirlwind of feelings.

He grins, his hand finding mine. "Just the start, Tory. There's a lot more where that came from."

After the zoo, we decide to make the most of our day in the city. Maksim, ever the planner, has a few tricks up his sleeve, and Adelina's bubbling excitement is contagious.

"Okay, team," Maksim announces with a grin that's too charming for his own good, "next stop, Millennium Park. Ever seen your reflection in a giant bean?"

Adelina bounces on her toes. "A giant bean? Like, for real?"

I laugh, caught up in the fun. "It's like a giant, shiny jelly-bean, but way cooler."

The Bean, or Cloud Gate if we're being formal, doesn't disappoint. We take turns making faces at our distorted reflections, and Maksim captures the moments with his phone, the perfect mix of tourist and doting dad.

Lunch is an adventure all its own. "Deep dish pizza," Maksim declares, and who am I to argue with a Chicago staple?

Sitting at a downtown pizzeria, we dive into a pie so loaded, it's practically a cheese fortress. "This is pizza?" Adelina eyes it suspiciously but is quickly won over after the first gooey bite.

"Bet you've never had it like this before," I tease, watching her try to navigate the cheesy labyrinth.

Maksim chuckles, wiping sauce from the corner of her mouth. "Chicago doesn't do pizza by halves."

The next stop finds us at Navy Pier, riding the Ferris wheel and playing carnival games. Maksim proves his mettle, winning Adelina a stuffed bear almost as big as she is. "Daddy's got skills," Adelina boasts, hugging her prize.

"Impressive," I admit, grinning at Maksim. "You planning on joining the carnival circuit?"

He winks and whispers to me, "Only if they accept mobsters with a knack for ring toss."

As the day winds down, I can't help but feel a warmth spreading through me. This is a glimpse into a life I could get used to. Laughter, silliness, and a side of Maksim that's utterly endearing.

Walking back to the car, Adelina's bear in tow, I catch Maksim's eye and smile. "Today was perfect."

He takes my hand, squeezing gently. "It's not over yet."

Back home and post-ice cream, we sink into the couch. Maksim hands the remote to Adelina with a flourish. "Your pick, Princess."

Her eyes light up, decisive. "Moana! It's about the ocean and adventures!" she announces, her excitement palpable.

"Moana it is," Maksim declares.

Movie night magic wraps around us, but like all good things, it eventually winds down. As the credits roll and Moana's journey concludes, Adelina starts her campaign for "just a little more time."

"But Tory's only here one more night! I need more time!" she pleads, her bargaining skills in full force.

Maksim remains firm yet gentle. "Time for bed, Princess. We've got a big day ahead."

The farewell hug Adelina gives me could melt the coldest heart, full of warmth and a touch of bedtime rebellion. With a resigned sigh, she heads upstairs, Maksim trailing behind her for the nightly ritual.

He pauses, casting back a look filled with silent promises. "Meet me in my bedroom," he suggests, or does he order... The way he says it promises worlds of delight.

Maksim's bedroom is a realm of understated luxury, a sanctuary that mirrors the man himself. The centerpiece, a king-sized bed with elegant posts at each corner, hints at possibilities that send a thrill through me. As I look around the room—its rich, dark woods and soft, ambient lighting—I toy with the idea of undressing, of waiting for him in a way that would make his return unforgettable.

But the thought of Adelina possibly making a last-minute appearance halts me. What if she convinces him for one more good night?

So, when Maksim enters, closing and locking the door behind him with a definitive click, I'm still clothed, but the anticipation crackles between us. His gaze, intense and laden with silent promises, sweeps over me, igniting that now-familiar tingle.

"Do you trust me?" he asks, his voice a low caress that somehow deepens the flutter in my stomach.

The question catches me off guard, not because I doubt him, but because it's loaded with the weight of what's unspoken. "Yes," I answer, my voice steady despite the hurricane of emotions his presence stirs within me.

"I want to try something new," he says, and his tone, coupled with the glint in his eye, tells me this night will be unlike any other.

"What do you mean?" I find myself asking, curiosity mingling with a slight edge of apprehension. The anticipation of stepping into uncharted territory with Maksim is thrilling yet daunting.

He leans closer, his voice a low, enticing whisper. "I want to surprise you," he begins, his words painting pictures of shadows and whispers, of a dance on the edge of our mutual trust and desire. "I want to introduce you to some of my unique tastes involving dominance and submission."

The words hang in the air between us, a proposition that's both intriguing and slightly intimidating. Part of me is wary, aware of the gravity of what he's suggesting. Yet, the larger part of me—the part that trusts Maksim implicitly—is captivated by the idea of exploring these depths with him.

"It's merely an extension of the things we've already done," he continues, seeing the hesitation in my eyes. "Just elevated."

"Elevated," I repeat, the word rolling off my tongue as I try to wrap my mind around the concept. The thought of venturing into this new aspect of our relationship with

Maksim—of surrendering and commanding in turns, of exploring the dynamics of power with him—holds a certain allure.

"I have no clue where to start," I confess, my nerves tangling with excitement.

His grin is wicked, like he's been waiting just for me to say that. "Why don't we kick things off with a kiss?" he suggests, his voice wrapping around me like velvet. That sounds perfect to me, a solid starting point in familiar territory.

He steps in close, erasing any space between us. When his lips find mine, it's like a spark setting off a whole fireworks show. The kiss is deep, passionate, a kind of conversation without words. It's all the reassurance I need, his hands gently yet firmly holding me to him, saying more about our connection than words ever could.

When he finally pulls back, leaving me all kinds of breathless, I'm hit with this wave of readiness. Whatever he's planning, whatever this new adventure is, I'm all in.

"So what comes next?" I ask, still feeling the echo of his kiss.

He takes his time answering, finding a seat in a nearby chair first. The way he looks at me, with intensity and a hint of something more, thrills me. "Undress for me," he says, his voice steady but laced with anticipation.

I start to, a bit awkwardly, and notice he's trying to stifle a chuckle. "What?" I ask, halfway between amused and self-conscious.

"It's just," he starts, and I can tell he's holding back more laughter, "you're undressing like you're in a changing room at the mall. Try doing it slower, more sensually."

His comment, far from offending, sparks a challenge within me. I take his advice to heart, turning the simple act into a slow reveal. His approval is evident in his eyes, that look of awe and admiration making me feel like the most captivating person in the world.

My eyes locked on his, I slip out of my clothes, taking them off slowly until I'm down to nothing but my bra and panties. As always, his gaze, the way he looks at me like I'm the sexiest thing he's ever seen in his life, makes the self-consciousness melt by the moment.

I reach behind me, undoing the clasp of my bra and slowly, teasingly sliding the straps down my shoulders. I love the way he looks at my breasts, the way he shifts in his seat as arousal takes hold. As I stand there, I imagine his cock pulsing to life, stiffening with each moment he looks at me.

Feeling bold and a bit daring, I decide it's his turn. "Your move," I say, my voice tinged with both confidence and playfulness.

He stands, accepting the challenge with a grin. His approach is measured, deliberate, a dance of shadows and light as he joins me in this game of reveal and conceal.

And then, in a moment of pure control, he reaches around me, giving my rear a hard swat. I gasp, that now familiar mixture of pleasure and pain running through me. My pussy clenches, my panties soaked.

"I'm the one giving the orders here, my dear." His eyes flick behind me, to the four-post bed. "Go to the bed. Lie down on your back."

Something about his tone makes him irresistible, his commands making my heart race. I do as he asks, walking slowly, letting him savor the sight of my nakedness. Once at the side of the bed, I lay down slowly on it.

Maksim approaches, standing at the side. He looks me up and down. With a jerk of his head, he tells me, "Grab the posts behind you."

I do, and he opens a bedside drawer and takes out black fabric he uses to bind my wrist to the posts, one after another. He ties the fabric expertly, making sure I'm good and bound, but not tying it tightly enough to hurt. Once my wrists are bound, he repeats the process with my ankles.

It's strange. I'm totally restricted, which you'd think would make me freak out, make me want to get free as soon as I could. But instead, I feel something different. I feel a surrender that excites me beyond what I thought possible.

Maksim rolls up his sleeves as he approaches the end of the bed. Once there, he put his hands on his hips and grins.

"Now, *devushka* – are you ready to begin?"

CHAPTER 24

TORY

I'm ready. So goddamn ready I can hardly think straight. My whole body is tingling with excitement, and all I want is for Maksim to take me, to claim me.

His eyes trail up and down my nude body as he makes his way slowly, so slowly, like the world is operating on *his* time, over to me. Once he's at the side of the bed, he reaches over to my panties and grabs the side of them. With a quick tug, he effortlessly tears the fabric and pulls them off.

I gasp and grin. "What would you say if I told you those were one of my favorite pairs?"

He shoots a grin of his own back at me. "I'd tell you your panties are the last thing that should be on your mind when you're with me."

My pussy clenches at his words. Thankfully, he doesn't make me wait for long. He reaches forward with his right hand once again, this time placing his hand between my thighs. He squeezes the sensitive flesh of my inner thighs, moving up until he reaches my center. I close my eyes, focusing on the sensation of him spreading me open, his fingertip touching my clit.

"Oh... *oh*..." The words slide out of me and I start squirming.

"Tell me how it feels when I touch you like this, *devushka*. How does it make you feel to know that whatever happens now, happens because I say so?"

I moan, focusing on his touch, the heaviness of his voice.

"I can bring you to the edge of pleasure and leave you there, and you wouldn't be able to do about it."

He's right. Maksim has proven himself to be a total tease. He increases the tempo of the slow circles he makes around my clit. There's no doubt in my mind he's well aware of exactly how to touch a woman to make her feel this way, to bring her to the brink of release and hold her for as long as he wants.

"What should I do, *devushka*?" He slides a finger inside me, making me squirm even more, the pleasure feeling like a spiral into which I'm falling deeper and deeper and deeper. "Do you wish to speak up? Or are you a little occupied?"

The pleasure is so intense by this point that I can barely think straight. All the same, part of me wants to smack him for being such a tease. God, he knows just how to push my buttons and has zero compunctions about playing me like a fiddle.

"You look like you're not in a mood to make decisions."

He's right. I'm moaning, squirming, thrashing at the restraints from the intensity of what he's doing to me.

"Allow me to make it for you."

He gives me the release I crave. His fingers still working in and out of me, he applies just the right amount of pleasure on my clit in exactly the right way. I release, the orgasm rushing through my body, my back arching, an *oh... FUCK!* exploding from the depths of my lungs.

The orgasm finishes, and he slows his pace, taking his hand away.

"Wonderful," he says. "You're a beautiful woman. But you're even more beautiful when you come. Touching you like this... I have to admit I'm somewhat selfishly motivated – it gives me the best view of your climax."

I catch my breath, my chest rising and falling. "Please Maksim," I say. "I need you inside me."

He shakes his head, that sexy, knowing smile still painting his features. "That will happen – don't worry. But for now, it's all about you."

To make his point, he brings his right hand to his mouth, placing the fingers that had been inside me past his lips. "Delicious," he says once he's licked them cleaned. "Almost sinfully sweet. Makes me want to taste even more."

A shudder of total delight runs through me as I realize where he's going with this. Maksim then reaches for my wrist restraints, loosening them just enough to give slack. I'm still bound, but there's more length for me to move. Once that's done, he returns to the edge of the bed. Maksim repeats the process with my ankle restraints. Then he takes me by the legs and pulls me toward him, my legs hanging off the bed, his mouth at precisely the level of my pussy.

He then leans forward, kissing my legs, moving up, lifting my legs and draping them over his shoulders. His nearness gives him the perfect positioning to bring his lips to my inner thighs, and then...

"Yes... yes, yes, *yes*."

It's all I can think to say as his mouth makes contact with my lips. He kisses me slowly and deeply, savoring me in just the way I imagined he would from how he'd tasted his fingers.

"Like heaven," he says, lifting his face from between my legs.

I close my eyes and moan, running my hands through his hair and holding him in place, the slack from the restraints giving me just enough movement to do so. The sound of his tongue against me fills the air, and by the time he slips his finger into me again, I'm ready for another release.

"Come for me," he says, his fingers rhythmically pushing inside. "Come for me right now."

He places his mouth on my clit again, pressing with his tongue. The sensation is enough to elicit another orgasm, and my whole body shakes as he eats me through it.

"That was... that was..." I can hardly speak. The two orgasms have reduced to me to an almost trance-like state where I feel like I'm on some crazy, mind-bending drug.

Maksim's mouth is curled on one side, and he's already slipping out of his clothes. I savor each new glimpse of his body, from his powerful build to his perfect ass, to the gorgeous and mysterious tattoos that decorate his skin.

"Tell me, *devushka*," he says. "How are you liking this glimpse into my tastes?"

I take a few more deep breaths before replying. "It's making me want more than a taste. I want a whole damn meal."

"There will be more than enough time for us to feast one on another."

Once he's down to nothing but his boxer-briefs, his cock straining against the fabric, Maksim reties my restraints, putting me back into the X form, my arms and legs spread. He climbs onto the bed, pulling down his underwear and exposing that gorgeous, thick prick of his. He's hard as I've ever seen him, the glistening tip of his head making me well aware of just how turned-on the teasing has been for him, too.

He positions himself, between my legs, getting on his knees and slipping a pillow under my rear, angling me up toward him. Then he places his head between my lips, clamps his hands down on my thighs, and pushes inside.

As I feel his manhood drive into me, splitting me in two, I realize right away the appeal of Maksim's tastes. The anticipation, the build-up, the feeling of being powerless and totally in at the mercy of another... it elevates the sensation of him finally taking me to another level.

I don't have to worry about moving, about anything other than focusing on how it feels as he stretches me, bottoms out inside me. The position is heavenly, Maksim's muscular body there for me to enjoy.

"You taste like heaven, you feel like heaven, you *look* like heaven," he says. "You know what that makes me think?"

"Tell me."

"Makes me think you're a goddamn angel."

Once more, I'm on the verge of melting. His cock buried and still inside, he caresses me, moving his big hands over my middle, my breasts, my shoulders. When his touch returns to my legs, he pulls back and drives into me again. I nearly shriek from the intensity, bucking my body hard into his.

We're soon in a perfect rhythm, Maksim making love to me like no man ever has before.

"Fuck," he groans, giving me another body-rocking pump, his powerful muscles flexing and tensing. "You have no idea how much I want to see you come again, *devushka*. I want to hear you moan, want to see you arch, want to see you leaking onto my sheets."

His words, his touch, his body, his *everything*... I can hardly hold back any longer. I open my eyes just enough to watch his thickness glide into me one more time, and then I release.

"*Oh... oh fuuuck!*" My screams fill the room, and all I can do is lay there underneath Maksim as his slow, deep thrusts bring me to another thundering orgasm. He joins me for this one, a guttural groan called up from the deepest reaches of his body erupting as his cock drains inside me.

I can feel his warmth, feel his cock pulse, feel every hard muscle of his body tense one last time as he climaxes, as we come together. Maksim holds for a moment, his huge chest expanding and contracting, his gorgeous body covered in sweat.

As we come down from the highs of our intense moment together, Maksim's back to being the gentle guy I'm crazy about. He loosens the ties, letting my arms flop to the sides.

He snuggles up beside me, pulling me into a hug that feels like home. My head finds its favorite spot on his chest, listening to his heart beat like it's tapping out a message just for me. His hand runs up and down my back in a way that's both soothing and kind of ticklish.

Right there, all wrapped up in Maksim, it hits me hard—I love this man. It's as clear as day, a truth that lights up everything inside me.

I'm caught in this push and pull of wanting to shout it from the rooftops and also wanting to keep it close, sacred. Telling Maksim I love him feels huge, like once those words are out there, everything changes. It's not that I'm scared he won't say it back. It's more about how big and real saying "I love you" feels.

Maybe, just maybe, when I'm ready to tell him, it'll just slip out as easy as breathing. Because with Maksim, everything just feels right.

CHAPTER 25

MAKSIM

Waking up on Sunday, there's this unfamiliar ache in my chest, a tightness that's hard to shake off. Tory's supposed to head back to her place today, back to that cramped space she calls home behind her shop. The thought alone gnaws at me. She deserves so much more than a fold-down bed in a room barely bigger than a closet.

Lying there, watching the soft rise and fall of her chest as she sleeps peacefully, I'm struck by how right she feels next to me. There's a serenity to her presence, a calm that seeps into my bones, chasing away the usual restlessness that marks my days and nights.

Adelina's taken to her in a way I've never seen before. My little girl has opened up like a summer flower under Tory's care. They laugh, they play, and there's a light in Adelina's eyes that's been missing for too long.

And me? I'm as gone for Tory as Adelina is. There's no denying it, no pushing it aside. She fits, in every way that counts. In her, I see everything I never knew I was looking for. But damn, is it too soon to voice that, to ask her to consider making this arrangement something more permanent?

I know she's wary, still holding back because of the shadows that trail my life, the dangers that weave through the fabric of my existence. I can't blame her; hell, I'd be wary too if our roles were reversed.

Maybe another month, then. Give her time to see that despite the chaos, the risks, we can make this work. Show her I can keep the darkness at bay, that I can be the man she needs, the father Adelina deserves, and the partner she might one day want.

As she stirs beside me, a sleepy smile gracing her lips as her eyes flutter open, I'm resolved. I'll wait, I'll prove myself, and when the time's right, I'll lay it all out. I'll ask her to stay, not just for a night, or a weekend, but for the unpredictable, promising future that awaits us.

For now, though, I'll hold her close, savoring the warmth of her body against mine, and let the morning stretch on a little longer. There's no rush in this moment, just the quiet promise of what could be, of what I'll fight to make a reality.

As Tory snuggles closer, a part of me wants nothing more than to wake her with a kiss that promises much more. Just a glance at her body is enough to make me rock hard, ready for a repeat of last night. But the sweet melody of Adelina's singing from her room drifts to my ears, derailing my thoughts. With a silent promise for later, I carefully extricate myself from the bed and dress quietly.

I tap lightly on Adelina's door, pushing it open to find her arranging her stuffed animals into what looks like a classroom setting. "Morning, sunshine," I greet her, earning a beaming smile.

"Papa! You're up early!" Her enthusiasm is as bright as the morning sun.

"I was thinking," I start, leaning against the door frame, "how about we make breakfast in bed for Tory? We haven't cooked together in a while."

Her eyes light up at the idea, the stuffed animals momentarily forgotten. "Yes! Can we make omelets? With lots of veggies and cheese?"

"Sounds perfect," I agree, and her excitement is infectious. Together, we head to the kitchen, our mission clear.

As we gather the ingredients, Adelina chatters about the different veggies she wants to include. "Tomatoes, bell peppers, onions, and don't forget the cheese," she dictates, taking her role as sous-chef very seriously.

I nod, amused and heartened by her enthusiasm. "Understood, Chef. Let's get cracking."

The kitchen soon fills with the sounds and smells of cooking, a symphony of sizzling and laughter as we work side by side. It's moments like these, simple and full of love, that remind me of what's truly important.

As the omelets near completion, I glance at the clock. "Let's make sure we get this to Tory before it gets cold," I suggest, plating our culinary creation with a flourish.

Adelina beams, proud of our teamwork. "She's going to love it!"

Adelina and I are putting the final touches on the breakfast tray when Irina breezes into the kitchen, her return catching me a bit off guard.

"Back so early, Irina? Planning to shoo us out of your kitchen?" I tease, arching an eyebrow.

Irina tosses her head back, her laughter mingling with the morning's cheer. "I should've known leaving you two in charge would turn my kitchen upside down. What's the special occasion?" Her gaze flits between the meticulously prepared tray and Adelina's excited face.

"We're making breakfast in bed for Tory," Adelina chimes in before I can reply, her grin spreading from ear to ear.

Irina shakes her head, mock disapproval written all over her face. "And here I thought I'd come back to a quiet house. Silly me."

Our banter is cut short by a strange noise—a soft thud, like something hitting the ground outside. "Hold that thought," I say, putting down the spatula. "I'll be right back." I cast a quick look upstairs, hoping the noise hasn't disturbed Tory's sleep. She deserves a few moments of peace, especially with the day we have planned.

As I make my way to the front door, the protective instinct kicks in, sharpening my senses. Adelina's laughter fades behind me, replaced by the quiet focus that comes with years of dealing with unexpected situations. Opening the door, I step out, ready for whatever or whoever might be waiting.

I scan the early morning quiet, finding nothing amiss. Yet, the stillness doesn't reassure me. Something about it sets off an alarm in the back of my mind, a reminder that peace is often fleeting in my world.

Charlie and Nick, the new hire, the men part of my security detail, make their rounds, visible signs of the ever-present watch over my domain. They spot me and offer a casual wave. I don't return the gesture, my mind too preoccupied with the heavier weights I carry.

Turning away from the door, my thoughts shift, unbidden, to the recent clash with Aleksey and the overhanging tension with my father. It's a thorn in my side, a problem that refuses to stay buried. Aleksey, with his ambitions and sharp tongue, has stirred the pot once too many, crossing lines that even in our world shouldn't be crossed.

The meeting at my father's, intended to clear the air, left more unsaid than resolved. My father, the old lion, still thinks he can command obedience and smooth over the fractures with a word. But some fissures run too deep, widened by betrayal and the harsh truths of power.

As I pull away from the window, the resolve settles in. This isn't just about squabbles within the family anymore. It's about protecting what I've built, what I cherish. Tory and Adelina represent a future I'm fighting for.

The warmth of the kitchen calls me back. For now, I'll play the part of the doting father, the attentive lover, even as my mind works through strategies and plans.

In this world, you're always playing the long game. And I intend to win, for their sake, for our future.

CHAPTER 26

TORY

Waking up, there's an undeniable grin plastered on my face, feeling like I've been wrapped up not just in these sheets, but in Maksim himself. It's kind of wild, the way his scent lingers, a comforting, strong embrace all its own.

Lying here, I can't help but replay bits and pieces, each memory sparking a fresh wave of butterflies. It's a new side of me, one that Maksim's somehow coaxed into the light, and I'm not mad about it. Not one bit.

I roll over, my hand instinctively searching for the warmth where Maksim lay just a short while ago. There's something about the residual heat that feels like a hug, a promise of his presence. I keep the dopey grin off my face, feeling every bit the love-struck fool. It's ridiculous, how much I want to stay tangled up in him, not just in these sheets, but in this life, in everything.

I shift, getting comfortable on my stomach, my gaze settling on the gentle dance of flames in the fireplace. The crackle and pop of the fire are soothing, almost hypnotic, providing the perfect backdrop for my thoughts to wander.

This weekend has been an eye-opener in so many ways, revealing layers of Maksim I hadn't dared hope to find. Seeing him with Adelina, witnessing the tenderness, the effortless love... it's confirmed so much for me.

I'd had this nagging doubt, this question mark looming over the whole situation with the baby. But now, watching the play of light and shadow, feeling the warmth of his bed, I know. I have to tell him. The fear of how he might react, of the potential perils his world could pose, is dwarfed by the certainty that he's a good man, a good father. And somehow, someway, we'll navigate this together.

The sounds of laughter and morning chaos drift up from the kitchen, Maksim, Adelina, and Irina all contributing to the symphony of a lively household. It's a music I'm growing fonder of by the minute, a total contrast to the solitude I'm used to. With a smile tugging at my lips, I dart into the bathroom for a quick shower, the warm water a welcome embrace.

As the steam wraps around me, my hand drifts to my belly, a gesture that's becoming more instinctual by the day. There's a surreal quality to it, this knowledge that I'm carrying a new life inside me. Excitement bubbles up, tinged with a healthy dose of fear. The reality of becoming a mom is daunting, thrilling, and a thousand other emotions I can't quite name.

Showered and dressed in a rush of newfound energy, I'm practically buzzing to get back to them, to immerse myself in the warmth of their company. But as I make my way downstairs, a draft catches my attention—the front door, inexplicably ajar.

Frowning, I approach, a sliver of unease slicing through the morning's joy. I push the door open wider, peering out into the bright day, searching for any sign of why it was left open. The quiet street offers no answers, just the peaceful hum of a typical morning.

With a shrug, I dismiss the nagging worry, attributing it to forgetfulness, maybe Irina or Maksim stepping out briefly.

Just as I step outside, soaking in the calm of the morning, a chill runs down my spine. Something's off.

Before I can turn, a hand like a vise clamps around my wrist, yanking me backward. Instinct kicks in—I try to pull away, but it's like being caught in a bear trap. I barely catch a glimpse of the assailant before his other hand slams over my mouth, and suddenly, I'm in a world of trouble.

My heart's pounding so hard I swear it might break through my rib cage. Panic's clawing at me, and I'm suddenly yanked out into the daylight that's become harsh and shadowy, making everything look sinister. The rough hand clamped over my mouth silences me before I can even scream. I'm fighting, kicking, and twisting, trying anything to get free, but it's like I'm battling a freaking iron statue.

Then, I'm off my feet, dangling in the air like some damsel in a bad movie, except there's no hero coming to save me. This dude's strength is just unreal. He's hauling me to a car, and I see the trunk open, ready to swallow me whole. *Hell no.* I'm not going out like this. I thrash harder, desperation giving me a boost of strength, but it's like trying to fight a tidal wave with a spoon.

Dumped in the trunk, the cold hits me hard, and that slam of the lid is like the final nail in a coffin. But I'm not giving up. Maksim, Adelina, the little life inside me—everything flashes before my eyes, and hell, if I'm not fighting for them.

The engine roars, and I'm trying to keep my cool, trying to think despite the fear. But panic grips me tighter than any physical chain could. I start kicking and punching the lid with all I've got, my screams tearing through the cramped darkness. For a second, there's this sliver of hope that someone will hear, that this nightmare will end as suddenly as it began.

Forced to face the reality that no one's going to hear me, I try to calm the storm inside. *Deep breaths, Tory, deep breaths,* I tell myself, trying to push away the terror. The car's moving further and further away from Maksim with every moment that passes.

Kicking the trunk is useless. I've seen enough movies to know the trick, but it's not working. It's like this car's built to keep nightmares inside. So, I stop, conserve my energy. I've got to think, got to be smart about this. There has to be another way out, another way to get back to Maksim and Adelina. And I'm going to find it, no matter what.

The music's blasting so loud outside this metal coffin, it's a wonder I can keep a single thought straight in my head. But I've got to focus, got to dig deep into my memory of the self-defense class I'd taken when I'd first moved out on my own. The instructor told us car trunks have an emergency release button inside.

Fumbling around in the darkness, my hands search desperately for the latch I'm sure is supposed to be here. But my hands come up empty, no latch, no lever, nothing. Maybe the car's too old, or maybe not every car has one. Great, just my luck.

Next, I move to the back of the seats, thinking maybe there's a chance they fold down or there's some kind of release mechanism. But again, nothing. I'm trapped in a metal coffin. The realization sinks in—I'm stuck here until they decide to let me out, wherever and whenever that's going to be.

The thought sends a fresh wave of panic through me, but I clamp down on it. I can't afford to lose it. Maksim has to notice I'm gone soon. He's smart, observant. The hope that he'll realize I'm missing, that he'll come for me, is the only thing keeping the despair at bay.

I curl into the fetal position, trying to conserve my energy, to prepare for whatever comes next. I have to be ready.

Time stretches into an endless void, each second an eternity in the suffocating darkness of the trunk. The car's movements become a monotonous rhythm, lulling me into a state of hyper-awareness where every sound, every shift feels amplified.

I try to piece together our route from the turns and stops, but without sight, it's like trying to solve a puzzle in the dark. Frustration gnaws at me, but I push it down, forcing myself to stay focused, stay sharp.

The car slows, the music cuts off, and the world outside falls silent. My heart leaps into my throat. This is it. We're stopping. Panic and anticipation twist inside me, battling for dominance. I take a deep, steadying breath, trying to brace myself for what's to come.

The engine shuts off, and for a moment, there's complete silence. Then the sound of car doors opening and closing pierces the quiet, followed by muffled voices. I strain to listen, to catch any clue or hint of where we might be, but the words are indistinct, the conversation frustratingly out of reach.

Suddenly, light floods the trunk as the lid is thrown open, blinding me after hours in darkness. Blinking against the brightness, I see figures looming over me, their faces obscured. I'm momentarily frozen, the shock of the transition from dark to light disorienting me. But then survival instinct kicks in. This might be my only chance.

Hands reach in to drag me out and I kick, aiming for any part of them I can reach.

"Not without a fight," I hiss through gritted teeth. There's a moment of surprise from my captors, a hesitation I use to my advantage, twisting and turning in an attempt to break free.

As they grapple to regain control, their hands rough and insistent, I feel the cold bite of something binding my wrists. Panic surges anew, lending me a burst of desperate strength. I twist, fighting against their hold with every ounce of my being.

In the chaos, my fingers find purchase on something unexpected—the edge of a mask. With a sharp tug, the mask peels away, and the face beneath is revealed in a moment of startling clarity.

Nicky. My heart stops. Nicky, of all people. His eyes widen in shock, mirroring my own, before a veil of resignation falls over his expression. Before I can process the betrayal, a cloth is thrown over my eyes, plunging me back into dark-ness, the reality of his involvement a bitter pill I have no time to swallow.

They work quickly now, their movements efficient, as if eager to rectify their momentary lapse. I'm hoisted once again, the world tilting around me as they toss me back into the trunk. This time, there's no fight left in me; bound and blindfolded, the feeling of helplessness is overwhelming.

CHAPTER 27

MAKSIM

A delina scrunches up her face, pushing the tiny espresso cup away with a dramatic shudder. "Yuck!" she exclaims, her expression one of utter betrayal.

I can't help but chuckle, having anticipated this reaction. "What? You don't like it?" I tease, already knowing the answer.

"It's gross!" she complains, wiping her tongue with the back of her hand as if she could erase the taste.

Irina, standing a safe distance away, leans against the kitchen counter with a smirk. "Maksim, you're playing with fire. Giving a child your rocket fuel could have unpredictable results."

I shrug, still amused by Adelina's exaggerated disgust. "It's just a taste. Not to mention, it's a rite of passage," I argue lightly. "Besides, after this, I doubt she'll want coffee again for at least another ten years. All part of the master plan."

Adelina, now recovered from her taste test, looks up at me with big eyes. "Can I have juice instead?"

"Of course, Princess," I say, ruffling her hair affectionately. "Irina, would you?"

Irina nods, already fetching a juice box from the fridge. "This should cleanse the palate," she says, handing it to Adelina, who takes it with both hands like a treasure.

"See? All is not lost. You've survived your first coffee," I tell Adelina, who's now sipping her juice with a satisfied air.

"Yeah, but no more," she declares, setting her terms.

"Deal," I agree, laughing. "No more coffee."

Adelina glances up as if trying to see the second floor. "Time to wake Tory?" she asks, as if she senses something's off.

I check the time, seeing that it's well past nine. "I think so," I agree, and prep a strong coffee for Tory, the kind that snaps you awake.

Coffee in hand, I head upstairs, but a cold draft stops me. The front door's wide open—an unmistakable sign of trouble.

My mind races to Tory. I abandon the coffee, storming toward the open door. "Tory!" I shout, eyes scouring the street for any sign of her, any clue.

Nothing. No guards. Just an eerie calm.

The instant chill of fear is unmistakable—a sharp signal that something's terribly wrong. My eyes dart in all directions, searching the quiet morning for anything out of place, but there's nothing. No one. Yet the open door screams danger louder than any alarm.

"Irina!" The urgency in my voice cuts through the stillness of the house. She's by my side in seconds, her expression flipping to alertness as she reads the situation in my eyes.

"Take Adelina to the safe room. Now," I command, my voice steel. "We might not be alone in the house." My mind races through scenarios, each more dangerous than the last.

"But, Tory—" Adelina's small, scared voice interrupts us. She's sensed the shift, the tension thick in the air.

"I'll find her, Princess." There's no time for explanations, no moment to comfort. "Irina, get her to safety," I repeat, firmer this time, my gaze locking with Irina's to convey the seriousness.

Irina doesn't hesitate. She nods, a silent agreement of the plan and swiftly lifts Adelina into her arms. Adelina's eyes, wide with fear, meet mine for a fleeting second before Irina turns, taking her away from the danger, away from the unknown.

As they disappear, a heavy silence settles over me. My heart pounds, not just with fear but with resolve. Whoever dared to breach my home, to threaten my family, will soon regret it.

I ease the door shut behind me, turning the lock with a quiet click. My heart's racing, but my hands are steady as I retrieve one of the guns from its hiding spot behind a nearby painting. The familiar weight of it in my grip brings a cold comfort.

From somewhere in the depths of the house, the heavy door of the secure room clicks shut. A wave of relief washes over me for a split second—Irina and Adelina are safe, out of harm's way. That's one less weight on my shoulders, but the danger's not over yet.

I move through the house slowly, every sense heightened, ready for any sign of an intruder. The silence is thick, broken only by my measured steps. The first floor reveals nothing, each room as empty as the next. But I can't relax yet; the second floor awaits.

Gun raised, I take the stairs, each step deliberate, bracing for what might come. The need to protect my family, to end this threat, sharpens my focus.

My heart's pounding as I head to the master bedroom, each beat loud against the silence of the house. I'm not sure what I'll find, but I can't help but throw a silent prayer to a God I'm not even sure I believe in. I hope to find Tory there, safe and asleep, and that I've overreacted. But every part of me is tensed for violence, gun raised, ready for anything.

I push the door open, my eyes scanning the room quickly.

The bed's empty. Tory's not here.

A heavy silence fills the room, and then, cutting through it, the distant rumble of a car engine fading into the distance. She's gone.

Heart slamming against my chest, I rush to the window, yanking the curtains open in time to see a strange car turn the corner and disappear. It's unfamiliar, not one I've seen before. Fingers tight around my phone, I dial my guards.

Silence. No one picks up. It's like they've vanished into the same void Tory has.

The room's a stark reminder of what's missing. Sheets rumpled from last night's escapade, her scent still clinging to the air, painting a picture of normalcy that's been brutally ripped away. I stand there, phone in hand, the echo of the car's rumble a taunting goodbye.

I'll do anything to get her back. Anything to protect Tory. This vow is a silent promise, not just to her, but to myself. Whoever has taken her has just started a war they won't win.

I check my gun, ensuring it's fully loaded and ready. The weight of it in my hand is a grim reminder of what I might have to do.

Reaching the side door, I open it cautiously and scan the surroundings. Nothing but stillness meets me, the silence almost taunting. I circle the house swiftly, every step calculated, my senses on high alert, ready to act at the slightest provocation.

Then, I freeze—a leg protrudes from the hedges. My grip tightens on the gun, my protective instinct, razor-sharp, ready to eliminate any threat.

Approaching the hedge, I discover the leg belongs to Charlie. He's grimacing, a bloody wound marring his head, struggling to sit up.

"What happened?" I demand, crouching beside him, my concern spiked with anger as I grab his arm and help him into a sitting position.

"Nick," he grunts, pain lacing his voice. "Hit me with his gun out of nowhere."

"Why?" My voice is cold, calculating, every word sharp with the promise of retribution.

Charlie shakes his head slightly, confusion and pain mingling in his expression. "Don't know. Aleksey sent him... to replace Ivan. Needed Ivan elsewhere."

The pieces aren't fitting together right. Aleksey, Nick, a sudden attack—it smells of betrayal.

I bark at Charlie to head straight to the safe room, to make sure Adelina and Irina are untouched by this chaos. Despite his injury, he nods, a pained expression on his face as he apologizes, clearly distressed by his failure to protect the house. His worry for what might come next is evident, but my focus is razor-sharp on the unfolding crisis.

Left alone, I whip out my phone, punching in Tory's number with a sense of urgency bordering on desperation. The familiar ringtone echoes through the house, a beacon guiding me to her phone abandoned on the kitchen counter, plugged into the charger, innocently blinking up at me.

The stark confirmation hits me like a punch to the gut— Tory's not here. The strange car I saw making its escape was carrying her away from me.

Rage floods my veins, a scorching torrent that demands satisfaction. They've dared to intrude into my life, to snatch away the woman I've come to love.

The knowledge that Tory was in the car, likely scared and alone, ignites a fury within me that's unmatched. Revenge isn't just a fleeting thought; it's a concrete plan. They will regret this day, regret ever thinking they could take something from me and not face retribution.

CHAPTER 28

Sitting at Maksim's kitchen counter, I'm hit by a beam of sunlight. It's kind of cinematic. Everything's bright, warm, and peaceful. I glance down, and whoa, my belly's massive.

Adelina's buzzing around, her energy like a little sunbeam of its own. She suddenly stops and looks up at me with those big, curious eyes. "Can you feel the baby kick?" she asks, her voice brimming with excitement only kids can muster.

I can't help but laugh, nodding. "Yeah, want to feel?"

Her face lights up, and she nods eagerly, inching closer. As she places her small hand on my belly, waiting, I love how these moments slow everything down. And sure enough, our little kicker decides to say hello, right on cue. Adelina's eyes go wide as saucers.

"Wow!" she gasps, and we share a look of both wonder and laughter.

Maksim saunters in, somehow looking like a million bucks in gray slacks and a shirt with the sleeves rolled up just so. He heads straight for the coffee, then turns to us with that smile.

"Ready for our day out, my two favorite girls?" he asks, all casual like we've been planning this for ages.

I'm sitting there, blinking at him because I don't remember any plans. Since when were we going anywhere? I've got this weird fog in my brain, making it hard to keep up. Meanwhile, Adelina's practically vibrating with excitement, bombarding Maksim with questions about what we're going to do.

Irina walks in, tossing a playful jab Maksim's way about forgetting his *third* favorite girl. We all laugh, but mid-giggle, a wave of dizziness hits me and I have to grab onto the counter. My head's spinning, and suddenly, the room feels way too warm.

As Maksim, Irina, and Adelina dive into their conversation, I'm feeling more off by the second. I make a move to stand, but my legs aren't having it. They're like jelly. I clutch the counter harder to keep myself from hitting the floor.

"Hey," I try, aiming for their attention, but my voice seems to vanish before it reaches them. They're wrapped up in their chat while I struggle to stay vertical.

Feeling a notch away from terrible, I raise my voice, "Guys!" Nothing. It's like I'm not even there. Panic starts to nibble at my edges because this isn't just feeling sick; this is wrong on a whole new level.

I'm yelling now, over and over, but it's like I'm invisible, mute. They're standing so close, but it's as if I'm far away. Something's really, really wrong.

Down I go, right to my knees, the kitchen swirling around me like a carousel gone wild. Maksim, Irina, and Adelina are still in their own world, their voices now twisting into sounds that don't make any sense to me, as if they've flipped to a language I've never heard.

I'm trying, really trying, to push myself up, to get their attention, to make them see me down here, but my body's just not cooperating. It's like my muscles have checked out, leaving me stranded on this spinning kitchen floor.

Then it's over, and I'm waking up to the lovely ambiance of a car trunk. I look around, getting my bearings, realizing I must've passed out.

Talk about a rough wake-up call. Every inch of me hurts, and I immediately go into mom mode, hands on my belly, freaking out over the little one in there.

Here in the dark, it's just me and my racing thoughts—and, of course, the baby. I'm trying to come up with some kind of plan, but honestly, it's like trying to nail jelly to the wall. I've got to believe Maksim's on the case, that his protective mode is going into overdrive. But as this car hums along, taking me who knows where, I'm left hanging with nothing but my worries, and this little life inside me, both of us heading into the unknown.

The car slows to a stop and my heart rate ticks up a notch. As the engine goes silent and footsteps signal someone's approach, my body kicks into a fight-or-flight mode that's all about fight right now.

As soon as the trunk cracks open, I'm a missile, launching myself at Nicky with all the grace of a stumbling toddler. We hit the ground in a tangle of limbs, my attempt at a heroic punch turning into a clumsy swipe.

"Really, Tory?" Nicky grunts, dodging my hand with a twist of his head, my palm barely grazing his cheek instead of smashing his nose.

I'm panting, furious. "You're going to pay for this, asshole."

He chuckles darkly, a sound that sends chills down my spine. "I'd like to see you try. Keep it up, and I'll break your jaw. Maybe that'll shut you up."

My heart's racing, adrenaline pumping. "You think you scare me?" I spit back, though my bravado is wavering.

"I should." He's looming over me now, the threat hanging in the air like a dark cloud.

I'm caught in the thick of it, my survival instincts clashing with the stark reality of my situation. Fighting Nicky seemed like a good idea for a hot second, but now? I'm in over my head, flailing in deep water.

Nicky grabs my arm, pulling me to my feet, intent on dragging me inside. Instinctively, I yank back. "Don't touch me," I snap, glaring at him.

He reaches for me again, and panic surges. I twist away, making a break for it, but he's too quick, grabbing me firmly. He raises his hand, and for a split second, I brace for the impact, but he stops himself. The air between us crackles with tension; it's clear he's not playing games.

"What the hell is going on?" I demand, trying to keep my voice steady. "Who the hell are you, Nicky?"

He lets out a frustrated sigh, his anger simmering just below the surface. "I worked some jobs with Ned," he says, as if that explains everything.

Ned. The name of my ex hits me like a ton of bricks. Nicky is just another criminal, a ghost from my past life with my ex, now haunting my present.

"So, what? You're a low-life crook just like him?" I can't hide the disdain in my voice.

Nicky's expression hardens. "I'm not the one you should be worried about," he warns, his tone icy. "There are bigger players in this game, Tory. And you're in deep."

Great. Just great. From one bad situation to a nightmare, courtesy of my stellar choice in men. Now I'm stuck with Nicky, the bridge between my messed-up past and this increasingly terrifying present.

His voice cuts through my thoughts. "Ned left a mess, Tory. A big one. People are still trying to clean up after him, and that loan? It's not going away."

Suddenly, it clicks. Nicky showing up at my business wasn't luck or happenstance. It was all planned. A cold realization washes over me—I've been a pawn since the start. My past with Ned is like a shadow I can't shake off, dictating my life without my say.

"Oh, and one more thing," he says, a grin spreading across his face. "Feel free to call me by my real name – Nicolai."

His voice is different, tinged with a slight Russian accent that hadn't been there before. The depths of his deception is clear – Nicky or Nicolai or whatever the hell his name is has been playing me from the start.

I'm seething inside, itching to lash out, to fight back against this manipulation. But reality hits. I'm not just responsible for myself anymore. There's a baby in the picture now. My instinct to protect my child overrides the fury, tempers the desperation.

As Nicky leads me, I take in our surroundings. The houses, grand and imposing, remind me of Maksim's place. We're in a neighborhood that feels eerily familiar, the architectural style mirroring Maksim's own home. Confusion and fear knot inside me.

"Where are we?" I demand, my voice tight with unease. "What are you planning?"

Nicky doesn't answer, his silence ominous. The pieces aren't adding up, and every step toward this house, so similar to Maksim's, plunges me deeper into a maze of questions. The sense of being trapped in someone else's scheme tightens around me.

Walking through this house with Nicky and his sidekick, I compare it to Maksim's. Where Maksim's place has a sort of elegant vibe, this house screams "trying too hard" with its over-the-top flashiness. It's like someone took the concept of luxury, dialed it up to eleven, and then threw in some glitter for good measure.

Maksim's home, for all its grandeur, feels lived-in, welcoming. You'll find Adelina's toys scattered around, her drawings on the fridge—signs of a real family. This place? It's like walking into a magazine spread for the rich and tasteless. I spot a staff of model-like women dusting and fussing over the decor, and guards that look like they eat nails for breakfast stationed at doors.

As they usher me upstairs, I'm taking in every detail, trying to make sense of where I am. The disconnect between this place and Maksim's home only adds to my confusion and unease. There's an impersonal, show-off quality here that sets my teeth on edge.

The procession stops at a door, and I'm led into a room that's as lavishly decorated as the rest of the house, but with a distinct lack of warmth. It's just so sterile, despite the opulence. I'm trying to keep a brave face, but inside, my anxiety is spiking. What's waiting for me here?

The moment I'm ushered into the office, it's like stepping onto the set of some alpha male fantasy. Everything screams overcompensation, as if the decor is trying to shout "I'm a man!" without a shred of subtlety. The walls are adorned with trophies and weapons, each one more aggressive than the last.

A massive desk of dark, polished wood dominates the room, looking more like a medieval banquet table than a place of work. Behind it sits a chair so unnecessarily large, it could double as a throne for a king with a serious inferiority complex.

And there's Aleksey, the man himself, perched behind that imposing desk like he owns the world. He's the embodiment of this room—trying too hard to project power and dominance. As he gestures for me to take a seat, I can't help but think of those nature documentaries where the animals puff themselves up to look bigger. This room, with its ludicrously macho vibes, feels like his version of puffing up.

Oversized paintings of lions and bulls reflect his false sense of pride, and the scent of rich, musky cologne permeating the air feels like a caricature of masculinity. It's as if he asked himself, "What would a stereotypical, douchey alpha male do?" and then did exactly that, but times ten.

Aleksey casually throws his feet up on his oversized desk, as if to underline the macho circus that is his office. He nods at the chair across from him, a smug smile playing on his lips.

"Take a seat," he says, his tone implying it's more of a command than a suggestion. "We've got a hell of a lot to talk about."

CHAPTER 29

I glare at Aleksey, my spine straightening. "I think I'll stand," I announce, not about to play into his little dominance game.

He laughs, a sound that grates on my nerves. "Seems Maksim hasn't trained you very well. He usually prefers his women a bit more obedient."

The audacity of the man! My temper flares, and I can't hold back. "Yeah? Well, fuck you," I shoot back, refusing to let him see just how much he's getting under my skin.

Aleksey's smirk doesn't waver. "Feisty. I like that. But it won't help you here."

I fold my arms, doing my best to seem unfazed, but inside, I'm boiling. This guy's pushing all my buttons, and we've barely started talking. "What do you want, Aleksey? Why am I here?"

He leans back, his casual demeanor in stark contrast to the tension zipping through me. "Straight to business. I like that, too. You're here, Tory, because of Ned's mess. And whether you like it or not, you're part of cleaning it up."

Part of me wants to keep lashing out, to break through his smug assurance with sharp words. But another part, the part that's whispering caution, reminds me I'm in a precarious position. I'm caught in a web I didn't weave, and anger won't get me out of it. Yet, giving Aleksey the satisfaction of seeing me cower? Not going to happen.

Aleksey doesn't seem offended. If anything, my behavior amuses him further. A thoughtful look crosses his face. "You know, Maksim wasn't always the charmer you see now. Oh no, he had quite the reputation back in the day."

I'm reluctantly curious, despite myself. "What are you talking about?" I ask, even though part of me screams to keep silent, to not give him the satisfaction.

"Let's just say he's made an example of more than one man who's crossed him." I feel a chill, despite the bravado I'm trying to maintain. Aleksey's eyes lock onto mine, ensuring I grasp the gravity of his tale. "He has a darkness in him, Tory. One he's done a good job hiding from you, it seems."

Aleksey leans back, his tale of Maksim's brutality hanging heavy between us. "You see, Tory, people like us, like Maksim, we're molded by the darkness. It's in our bones."

I try to keep my voice steady. "You're enjoying this, aren't you? Trying to freak me out with your stories."

He smirks. "It's not just stories, darling. It's a warning. You think you know Maksim, but there are layers to that man you haven't even begun to peel back."

THE ARRANGEMENT | 203

My skepticism must be evident because he continues, each word dripping with condescension. "Oh, you doubt me? Ask him about the warehouse on Fifth, ask about the fire. See if he tells you the sweet, bedtime version or the truth."

The mention of specific events sends a jolt of unease through me. "Why should I believe anything you say?" I challenge, even as a part of me dreads the answers to the questions Aleksey has planted.

"Because, Tory," he says, a cold hardness in his eyes, "ignorance in our world doesn't grant you safety; it makes you a target. And believe me, being in the dark with a man like Maksim is the last place you want to be."

"You're lying," I say, more out of defiance than conviction.

Aleksey shrugs, an infuriating smirk playing on his lips. "Believe what you want but know this—Maksim Morozov is not the saint you think he is. And you, my dear, are in the middle of a very dangerous game."

His words hang in the air, a threat veiled as advice. I'm left grappling with the uncertainty of it all, wondering how much of the man I care for is the person Aleksey describes, and how much is the one I've come to know.

Aleksey doesn't miss a beat, his voice smooth as he shifts gears. "I didn't bring you here just to give you a fright, Tory. I'm offering you a deal."

"A deal?" My voice is skeptical, incredulous at the turn this conversation is taking.

He nods, a predator's grin spreading across his face. "There's a storm coming to this city. A shakeup. And when the dust settles, I'll be the one standing tall. Maksim, on the other hand..." He lets the thought hang, unfinished but clear.

"And what? You want me to... what, exactly?" I'm struggling to keep up, to mask the rising horror at his implication.

"I want you, Tory. No point in dressing it up. You're smart, beautiful, and, let's face it, wasted on Maksim. This is your chance to align with the winner. With me." He leans closer, his gaze locking onto mine. "Think about it. You could be my queen. My favorite pet. Doesn't that sound enticing?"

The revulsion that surges through me is almost palpable. "Be your pet?" The word tastes foul, and I can barely contain the disgust. "You think I'd ever choose that? Choose you?"

Aleksey laughs, a sound devoid of humor. "Oh, gorgeous, it's not about choice. It's about survival. And trust me, in the war that's coming, you'll want to be on the winning side."

His assurance, his arrogance, it's all designed to intimidate, to coerce. But it only fuels my resolve, my disdain for the man before me.

"Listen, I don't know what twisted fantasy you've concocted in your head, but I'm not some prize to be won. I'd rather take my chances with Maksim in whatever hell you think you're going to unleash than spend another second entertaining this delusion of yours."

Aleksey's expression hardens, the facade of charm slipping to reveal the cold ambition underneath. "You're making a mistake. But don't worry," he adds, a sinister promise laced within his words, "since you've decided to align yourself with the wrong side, I have other plans for you. But I'll warn you, most women can't withstand my charms."

His confidence, his assumption of my inevitable capitulation makes my skin crawl. But it also clarifies one thing: whatever game Aleksey's playing, whatever future he envisions, I want no part in it. Not at his side. The very idea makes me sick.

Aleksey stands, and as he rounds the desk, a spike of fear shoots through me. I brace myself, half-expecting a blow, but what he does next is somehow even more revolting. He leans in close, too close, and inhales deeply, the air from his nose brushing against my hair.

"You're too beautiful for my brother," he murmurs, his voice a mix of mock pity and something darker.

The disgust rolls over me in waves, strong enough that I actually gag. "Keep away from me, or I swear I'll puke," I snap, my stomach churning in agreement.

He only chuckles at my threat, an irritatingly unperturbed sound. Shrugging, he signals Nicky with a lazy flick of his wrist. "Take her downstairs," he commands, as if discussing the weather rather than dictating my movements.

Nicky's grip is firm on my arm, but I'm too nauseated to resist effectively. As we start to move, Nicky hesitates, looking back at Aleksey. "Do you want Maksim shot on sight?" he asks, a hint of eagerness in his tone.

Aleksey pauses, a slow smile spreading across his face. "No, let him come. It'll be more fun this way," he decides, his gaze flickering to me with a glint of malice. "He'll show up, desperate and heroic. But he won't find what he expects."

"No!" I yell, my voice cracking with the intensity of my denial as his meaning sinks in. "Maksim is your blood, your brother. How can you even think about doing this?"

Nicky's grip on my arm tightens as he hisses, "Shut up," but I barely hear him over the sound of my own heart pounding.

Aleksey just laughs, a sound devoid of any warmth. "Oh, Tory, that's exactly why he needs to be taken out. Because he's my brother." His eyes gleam with a chilling resolve.

Tears sting my eyes as Aleksey steps closer once more. I try to back away, but Nicky's like a vise, keeping me anchored in place. "Maksim won't be taken out immediately," Aleksey continues, his voice smooth as silk and just as suffocating. "I want him to watch as I take everything he loves, piece by piece."

I'm frozen, horror rooting me to the spot. Desperation claws its way up my throat, and in a last-ditch effort to find some shred of humanity in him, I blurt out, "I'm pregnant, Aleksey. You're talking about your niece or nephew."

Aleksey pauses, and for a moment, I dare to hope my words have impacted him. But his expression hardens again, and any flicker of decency vanishes. "Even better," he says, his voice dripping with venom. "What a perfect way to bind you to me, Tory. Maksim's child, raised under my roof. Can you imagine the agony that would cause him?"

I'm shaking now, not just with fear, but with an overwhelming sense of betrayal and disgust. How could anyone, even someone as ruthless as Aleksey, be so cold, so cruel? Nicky's grip is the only thing keeping me upright as I struggle to process the depth of Aleksey's depravity.

Aleksey's eyes light up with a twisted sort of glee. "Does Maksim know you're pregnant?" His voice is eager, like he's just been handed the winning card.

I'm torn, caught between wanting to shield this truth from him and the instinct to be honest. In the end, the truth spills out. "No, he doesn't know yet."

Aleksey laughs, the sound echoing off the walls, chilling me to the bone.

"You're insane," I spit out, anger and fear mingling in my voice. "A complete psychopath."

He doesn't flinch at my words. Instead, he shrugs, as if I've complimented him. "Or maybe I simply kill you. Your death, and the death of Maksim's unborn child," he muses, "what a perfect way to break him."

I'm reeling, every instinct screaming at me to get away, to protect my baby from this madman. But before I can even think of a plan, Aleksey's issuing orders. "The basement," he says to Nicky, who immediately starts dragging me away.

I'm fighting every step, but Nicky's grip is like iron. As we leave the office, Aleksey's voice follows us, a promise or a threat, I can't tell which. "Don't worry, Tory. Nothing will happen to you until Maksim arrives."

His words hang heavy in the air, a dark cloud that follows me as I'm hauled down the hallway. The reality of my situation is suffocating, the danger I'm in, and the danger my baby is in, all too real. But amidst the fear, a fierce determination takes root.

Maksim doesn't know I'm pregnant, but I'll do everything in my power to protect our child from his brother's madness.

Somehow, I have to survive this—for me, for my baby, for Maksim.

CHAPTER 30

MAKSIM

I n the kitchen, the late morning light doesn't do much to soften the grim scene before me. Charlie's sitting there, a makeshift bandage wrapped around his head, looking like he's gone a few rounds with a heavyweight. The sight stirs a mix of anger and concern within me.

"What happened?" I ask, my voice calm, though inside, I'm anything but.

Charlie meets my gaze, guilt written all over his face. "Nicky got the jump on me. I didn't see it coming," he admits, his voice strained.

The part of me that's all raw instinct wants to lash out at him for letting his guard down, especially now, when every second counts and Tory's out there with God knows who. But I clamp down on that impulse hard. Getting mad at Charlie won't get me any closer to finding her.

"I'm sorry, Maksim. I should've been more alert," he continues, the apology hanging heavily in the air between us.

I take a deep breath, forcing myself to stay focused on what matters. "Look, Charlie, what's done is done. Right now, we need to figure out where they've taken her. Any idea why Nicky would do this?"

He shakes his head, wincing slightly. "No clue. But he mentioned something about Aleksey before he knocked me out. Sounded personal."

Aleksey. The name sends a chill down my spine, not because I'm afraid of him, but because of what he's capable of doing to Tory to get to me. It's a low blow, even for him.

As I'm about to head out, I notice Charlie swaying slightly, his balance off. The guy's clearly not in fighting shape, a second away from hitting the floor rather than an enemy.

"Charlie, you're in no condition to come with me," I state firmly, noting the frustration that flickers across his face.

"I want to help, Maksim. I owe you," he insists, his voice tinged with determination, but it's clear he's fighting just to stay upright.

"The best way you can help is by staying here," I counter. "I've called men to the house to protect Adelina and Irina. You tell them what's going on and watch over them until they get here."

Reluctantly, he nods, understanding the role he has to play. He grabs his iPad, linking up to the security cameras trained on the safe room. The screen shows Adelina and Irina, safe for now, a small comfort.

I lean toward the iPad's speaker. "I'm heading out, but I'll be back soon. Stay safe," I say, my voice more for Adelina than anyone else.

"Papa, I love you," Adelina's voice comes through the speaker, small and brave in the face of uncertainty.

A wave of emotion hits me hard. "I love you too, Princess. More than anything," I reply, the words thick in my throat.

Charlie, now firmly planted in front of the iPad, meets my gaze. "I'll guard them with my life, Maksim. They won't be alone."

Nodding, I clasp his shoulder briefly in gratitude and solidarity. Then, with no time to waste, I turn to leave, every step fueled by the promise of returning to those I love. The fight ahead is unclear, fraught with danger, but one thing is crystal clear: I will do whatever it takes to bring Tory home and keep my family safe.

My mind's already racing, plotting, planning. I'll tear through anyone who stands in my way. Aleksey wants a war? He's got one. But he's about to learn I don't play by the rules, especially not when it comes to the people I love.

As I drive to my father's place, my thoughts are a whirlwind, mostly circling back to Tory. The ache of her absence is a sharp, constant pang, reinforcing how deeply I've fallen for her. It's in these moments of fear and uncertainty that I realize just how much I need her in my life.

Pulling up to the house, the weight of what might come hangs heavy on me. Tiffany greets me at the door with her usual warmth. "Maksim, it's so good to see you! How's Adelina?" she asks, her smile genuine.

For a brief moment, I'm caught off guard by the normalcy of her greeting, and a wave of guilt washes over me. I'm possibly on the brink of confronting, maybe even having to take down, her son, my own brother, to save Tory. The thought is a bitter pill, one I'm not sure how to swallow.

"She's fine, Tiffany. But I really need to see my father. It's important," I manage to say, trying to keep my voice steady.

"Of course, he's in the kitchen eating breakfast. You know how he is about breakfast," she replies, stepping aside to let me through, unaware of the chaos brewing inside me.

Stepping into the kitchen, a calm envelops me. The familiar smells of brewed coffee and something sweet cooking on the stove mingle in the air. The room is bathed in the soft light of morning, casting serene shadows that dance quietly across the surfaces.

My father sits at the small nook by the window. The newspaper is spread out in front of him, his reading glasses perched at the end of his nose, marking him as absorbed in the world's stories beyond our immediate concerns. Beside him, a small plate of fresh fruit is arranged meticulously—Tiffany's influence, no doubt, steering him toward healthier choices.

He looks up as I enter. "Maksim! Come, have some breakfast. You look like you could use it," he gestures toward the inviting spread.

"I'm not here to eat, I'm here to talk about Aleksey," I state, then hesitate, feeling the heaviness of my situation. I notice the subtle shift in my father's demeanor. He sets his newspaper aside with a careful, deliberate motion and removes his glasses, placing them on the table. He sighs, a deep, knowing sound that fills the space between us.

"There was a time," he begins, his voice rich with the weight of memories, "when I found myself at odds with an old friend. It wasn't just business; it became personal, dangerously so. But no matter how heated things got, we never let it spill over to our families. That line was sacred."

My father's story unfolds as he leans back, a faraway look in his eyes. "This friend and I, we were thick as thieves, literally, in our younger days. But as we climbed the ranks, our visions for the future began to clash. It got ugly, my son. There were threats, fights... I feared it might end in bloodshed."

He pauses, his gaze returning to the present, to me. "One night, it came to a head. We found ourselves face to face, guns drawn. It could've been the end for one of us, or both. But then, he mentioned my wife, your mother, Maksim. Not as a threat, but as a reminder of what was at stake. Of who we were outside of this feud.

"The realization hit us both like a cold splash. We were willing to destroy everything we had, all for pride and power. In that moment, we chose to step back. It took time, and not all wounds healed, but we drew a line. Our families, our loved ones were off-limits."

I listen, absorbing not just the words but the gravity behind them.

"So, what happened to him?" I ask, curious despite myself.

My father smiles, a touch of sadness in his eyes. "Life happened, Maksim. We went our separate ways, but we kept that truce. He passed away some years ago, but I never forgot the lesson from that night."

The story settles over me, a parallel to my own struggle with Aleksey. The conflict, the potential for resolution—it's all there, a blueprint laid by the past.

"Father, I can't see such a way out with Aleksey. He's crossed a line I can't ignore," I admit, feeling the burden of my next words.

My father nods, understanding etched deep in his features. "I know, son. And I'm not saying you should back down. We protect our family, always. But remember, there's strength in choosing how to fight this battle."

The urgency of the situation makes it difficult to stay still. My father's observant eyes are on me, a quiet strength in his gaze. "I know you're not part of this, Father. You've always been straight with me."

"I know what I know. But you're correct. So, tell me, Maksim – what's going on with your brother?"

He nods, a signal for me to go on. So, I lay it all out—the abduction, Aleksey's threats, and his dark intentions for Tory. Sharing the details feels like unloading a burden, yet the weight of reality remains.

"I've fallen in love with her, Father. She's a part of my life, and Adelina's," I confess. "She's more than just a woman I'm seeing."

"I see." My father lets out a heavy sigh, a mix of concern and a certain weary disappointment. "I've sensed the growing rift between you boys, but this..." He shakes his head, clearly disturbed. "Dragging a man's family into business conflicts is cowardice. It's a boundary we never cross."

"Aleksey didn't just cross it; he's taken it to a whole new level," I reply, the frustration evident in my voice. "He's got Tory, and he's made it painfully clear he's willing to use her to get to me."

Hearing this, my father's demeanor shifts, a hardened resolve taking over. "Aleksey's always pushed the limits, but involving Tory, that's beyond the pale. We Morozovs, we have our principles, our honor. What he's doing isn't just an affront to you; it's against everything our family stands for."

I nod, the solidarity in his words bolstering me. "That's why I'm here. I need your help, Father. To get Tory back, and to deal with Aleksey. Before things get even worse."

There's a long look between us, one of understanding and agreement. "Of course. We'll sort this out. Aleksey seems to have forgotten the values we uphold, but we haven't. And we'll make sure he remembers."

The air in the kitchen becomes charged with a new energy as my father and I hunker down over the table, a makeshift war room. He starts, his voice low but firm, "First, we need to consider who we can trust. Aleksey's influence has spread, and we can't afford any leaks."

I nod, absorbing his caution. "I've got a few guys who've been with me through thick and thin. They're loyal. They're at the house watching over Adelina and Irina."

"Good," he approves, then moves on. "Now, potential hideouts. Aleksey's not a fool; he'll have taken Tory somewhere off the grid, somewhere he thinks we won't find."

I lean in, focused. "There are a few places I can think of that Aleksey's mentioned in passing. Old warehouses, a couple of secluded properties."

My father's eyes light up with strategic fire. "We'll need to scout them discreetly. And Maksim," he adds, a stern edge to his voice, "we must be absolutely sure before we make a move. The last thing we want is to tip Aleksey off or, worse, walk into a trap."

"Understood," I reply, feeling a semblance of control returning. The path ahead is fraught with danger, but with my father's guidance, it seems less insurmountable.

"And Tory," my father continues, his expression softening. "We have to consider her safety above all. Any action we take, we need to ensure it doesn't put her in further danger."

His emphasis on Tory's safety cements my resolve. "We'll get her back, Father. And we'll do it without giving Aleksey the satisfaction of seeing us break."

As the planning phase shifts into preparation for action, I glance at my father, the weight of our next steps heavy in the air. "There might be bloodshed," I admit, the reality of what lies ahead settling over me like a shadow.

My father meets my gaze squarely, the lines of his face etched with the hard wisdom of years. "I understand, Maksim."

The thought of Tiffany crosses my mind, her unwavering warmth and how this conflict could shatter her world. I can't bring myself to voice my concerns about her; the potential fallout is a wound too painful to probe. But there's another pressing need I can't ignore. "I need men. Trust worthy men – men ready right now."

He doesn't hesitate. "Take Viktor and Michael. They've been with me for years, loyal and steadfast. They've never sided with Aleksey, rejected his methods outright. You can trust them."

The relief at his quick decision is palpable. "Thank you," I say, the gratitude deep and sincere. I'm spared a goodbye to Tiffany, for which I'm silently thankful. The less she knows now, the better for her.

Viktor and Michael are already outside. I brief them on everything—Aleksey's actions, his threats, and what Tory means to me. Their reaction is immediate and decisive.

"Let's go get your woman," Viktor says, his voice firm, the determination clear in his eyes. Michael nods in agreement, his expression grim but resolute.

Aleksey has made a grave mistake, one he'll soon come to realize.

CHAPTER 31

TORY

I'm pacing back and forth like a caged animal in this basement room that's become my temporary prison. How long has it been? Twelve hours? A whole day? Without a clock, time's turned into this abstract thing that just stretches and folds on itself.

The door's bolted shut, solid and mocking any fantasy I have of a dramatic escape. I've given it the once over, twice over—no luck. No loose hinges to exploit, no overlooked tools lying around, and no windows I can crawl out of.

So, here I am, stuck, trying not to spiral into panic or despair. Maksim's out there, and if I know anything about him, it's that he's turning the city upside down to find me. That thought alone offers a sliver of hope in this dim, clockless room. I have to stay calm, stay smart, and wait for my moment.

In this spartan cell, there's one thing that actually catches my eye—a pool table. In the middle of my makeshift prison stands this relic of leisure, stripped of its felt and glamour, looking as out of place as I feel. But the object beside it really piques my interest—a lone pool cue, forgotten or perhaps left behind as some cruel joke by my captors.

I approach it cautiously, as if it might vanish the moment I acknowledge its existence. Picking it up, I'm struck by its heft, the solid feel of it in my hands. It's not exactly Excalibur, but in the absence of knights and swords, it feels pretty close. It could be a weapon, I muse, the thought both empowering and terrifying.

I take a few tentative swings, trying to mimic every action hero I've ever seen, hoping I don't look as ridiculous as I feel. The air swooshes quietly with each movement, the sound oddly reassuring.

The reality of my situation is stark—trapped with limited options and even less experience. But this pool cue, this unexpected ally, offers a sliver of hope, a means to fight back when the moment comes. And as I practice my swings, I feel a growing determination. I may not be ready to take on the world, but I'll be damned if I don't put up a fight.

There's a small slit in the door I hadn't noticed before in my attempts to find an escape route. Curiosity piqued, I tiptoe closer, the weight of the cue now feeling like potential, like opportunity.

The voices on the other side are muffled, the words indistinct, but there's no mistaking the bored tone of guard duty gripes. My fingers itch to reach through, to maybe catch a snippet of useful information, but the slit's too high, too narrow. Then it hits me—the cue.

Gently, with the sort of caution you'd use handling dynamite, I nudge the face of the slat open with the pool cue. It's a small victory, but the voices filter through more clearly now. One's unmistakably Nicky, his distinct accent carrying a mix of annoyance and impatience. The other voice, deeper, gruffer, belongs to what can only be described as typical goon material.

They're lamenting their current assignment—me, essentially. How babysitting duty's beneath them, how they'd rather be out there, in the thick of whatever nefarious plans they've got brewing.

"I wish we were doing anything more exciting than babysitting," the other guard grumbles, unaware of just how keenly I'm listening.

"Just wait," Nicky replies, his tone lowering into something more ominous. "There's going to be more than enough action for us in the next few days."

The other guard, obviously interested, presses him. "What do you mean?" His voice is rough, eager for a glimpse into the plan.

Nicky hesitates, a brief silence hanging in the air. "Aleksey said not to spill the beans," he admits, but the other's prodding seems to break down his resolve. "Alright, alright. Tory's here as bait. Aleksey's convinced that by taking her, he's thrown Maksim off his game, got him all emotional."

My heart skips a beat, the gravity of my situation sinking in even deeper with every word Nicky spills.

"He's planning to use her to draw Maksim into a trap, right here at Aleksey's house, where he'll be taken out. After that," Nicky's voice grows colder, "it's war. Maksim's crew will be wiped out, and Igor... Igor will be overthrown."

The other guard's chuckle sends a chill down my spine, their casual discussion of violence and betrayal echoing ominously in the cramped space. They're talking about an upheaval, about using me as the linchpin in a plan that could destroy everything Maksim and his father have built.

As I step back from the door, the pool cue suddenly feeling heavier in my hands, a potent brew of fear and resolve settles over me. They may see me as just a piece of bait, a pawn in their grand scheme, but I'm not about to sit quietly and let Aleksey's plans unfold. Maksim is out there, and if there's even the slightest chance he's coming for me, I need to be ready.

I'm no action hero, but standing here, holding this pool cue like it's my blade, I'm sort of forced into the role. I tuck myself behind the door, figuring if it swings open, I'll be hidden behind it.

I hear the other guard head out, then wait a few minutes... alright, it's showtime. I take a deep, not-at-all-calm breath and yell, "Hey, I could really use some water here!" Louder than I expected, my voice bounces off the walls, sounding way more confident than I feel.

Makeshift weapon in hand, my heart is doing the samba in my chest. I'm not looking to kill anyone, but if it comes down to protecting my little plus-one, you bet I'm going to swing this thing like I'm going for the fences.

Waiting for the door to open feels like an eternity, each second ticking by with my heart rate ratcheting up a notch.

Just when I'm starting to second-guess my whole strategy, the sound of a key turning in the lock snaps me back to the moment. *Alright, Tory, this is it—no more rehearsals.* I grip the pool cue with both hands, trying to channel every badass movie hero I've ever seen.

The door swings open, and there it is—an arm stretching into the room, a bottle of water in its grasp. Without a second thought, I swing the cue with all the might I can muster, targeting the arm. The impact sends the bottle flying, smashing against the floor, water splashing everywhere.

Nicky yells out—a yelp of surprise and pain that tells me I've hit my mark. But there's no time to celebrate; I'm already pulling the cue back for another go. I turn toward Nicky and aim higher; the cue connects with his chin in an upward swing. The look of shock on his face would be comical if the situation weren't so dire.

Not giving him a chance to recover, I swing one more time, harder, catching him at the back of the head. Down he goes, hitting the ground with a groan that tells me he won't be getting up anytime soon.

I stand there for a second, pool cue still in hand, staring at Nicky laid out on the floor. Part of me can't believe that actually worked.

There's no time to dwell on my newfound combat skills. I've got an escape to make and a warning to deliver. Still, as I step over Nicky, making my way out of the basement, I can't help but feel a tiny bit of pride.

With a quick, decisive motion, I slam the door shut and twist the key, locking Nicky on the other side. Who knew the guy would make it so easy for me? Key left in the door and all. I pause for just a second, taking in the silence of the basement. No sign of the other guard, thankfully. Looks like luck might actually be on my side for once.

I don't waste another moment, sprinting for the stairs. My heart's pounding like it's trying to break free from my chest, every step fueled by adrenaline and sheer will to get out. The thought of running into a locked door at the top sends a fresh wave of panic through me, but I push it aside.

Bursting into Aleksey's house from the basement is like entering enemy territory. The lavish decor that seemed so extravagant during the day now feels like a maze of shadows and potential hiding spots for the guards. It's nighttime, the cover of darkness both a blessing and a curse. I thank every lucky star that darkness is playing for Team Tory tonight.

Moving with caution, I channel every stealthy character I've ever admired. Each step is measured, each breath controlled. I make it halfway across the main hallway when I hear voices—Aleksey and his crew, by the sound of it.

My heart skips a beat, and I dive behind a wall, pressing myself as flat as possible. Peeking around the corner, I see them, Aleksey and his inner circle, too caught up in their discussion to notice me. The darkness, my unexpected ally, wraps around me, hiding me from their view.

They start talking again, and I'm all ears, hidden in my little nook of darkness.

Aleksey's voice slithers through the air. "When Maksim gets here, we'll play nice. Offer him a chat, a little heart-to-heart."

One of his goons, sounding way too excited for my liking, chimes in, "And then, when he's least expecting it—boom!"

Aleksey laughs, the sound sending shivers down my spine. "Exactly. He won't even see it coming. Tory's the perfect bait. After we take care of him, it's open season on my father and his crew."

The casual way they're plotting this, like they're discussing some twisted party plans, makes my stomach turn.

As they move away, their laughter echoing down the hall, I gather my courage. This isn't just about sneaking around anymore. It's about blowing Aleksey's plan wide open, saving Maksim, and getting the hell out of this house of horrors.

As I sneak through the dimly lit hallways of Aleksey's mansion, my heart is thumping wildly. Each door I try is stubbornly locked, increasing my panic with each failed attempt. With no other options, I race up the stairs, desperately hoping for an escape.

But the next floor is just as bleak and unwelcoming. I dash along the corridor, trying each window in turn, but they're all securely locked. My heart sinks deeper with each attempt, the walls seeming to close in around me, the air growing thinner with my rising panic.

Suddenly, the sharp shriek of an alarm pierces the heavy silence, freezing me in my tracks.

I'm caught.

The house erupts into a frenzy, lights flickering on, casting long, sinister shadows that reach out like fingers ready to ensnare me. My instincts kick in—I run, my breaths short and sharp, echoing the frantic pounding of my heart.

Rounding a corner, the ominous thud of boots coming up the staircase signals the approach of the guards. Desperation lends speed to my steps, but the hallway ends abruptly. I'm trapped. I whirl around, heart in my throat, as the guards appear, their guns raised and ready.

And there he is—Aleksey, emerging from behind them with a smirk that chills my blood. He steps forward confidently, his presence commanding and menacing. Nicky is with him, looking rough after my handiwork with the pool cue. Asshole must not have been completely knocked out.

"You've been a very bad girl, Tory," he says. His eyes lock on mine, a dark amusement in their depths.

CHAPTER 32

MAKSIM

As the city's lights streak by, casting fleeting shadows inside the car, I press the end call button on my phone, letting out a slow, deliberate breath. The conversation I've just wrapped up, laden with plans and contingencies, sits heavy in my thoughts.

Viktor catches my eye in the rearview mirror, his stoic demeanor tinged with curiosity. "Everything set?" he asks, his voice as steady as ever.

"Yes, it's all in motion," I reply, my tone even, masking the whirlwind of strategies and potential outcomes racing through my mind. I pause, reflecting on the call I just made, a conversation I never envisioned having. "You know, if you told me a year ago I'd be making that call, I would've laughed. Funny how things change."

Victor nods, understanding the depth of what's unsaid. The car hums quietly as we continue our drive, the anticipation building with each passing mile.

"We're heading into uncertain territory. You ready for what's waiting at Aleksey's?" Michael's question breaks the silence, pulling me back from my reverie.

I meet his gaze in the mirror again, my resolve firm. "I'm ready. Aleksey's estate is where this ends, one way or another. We have to confront him, even if we have to do it on his own turf."

The car slows as we approach the gates of Aleksey's mansion, and I brace myself for what's to come. The element of surprise I'd hoped for vanishes the moment we're met by guards, clearly forewarned of our arrival.

"He's expecting you. Go to the front door. Alone," one of the guards instructs, an edge of arrogance in his voice.

Stepping out of the car, I glance back at Victor and Michael, their loyalty unwavering. "Stay sharp," I tell them, my voice low. "No matter what happens, we see this through. But listen, if Tory comes out alone, you take her straight to my father. Make sure she's safe, no matter what."

Approaching the mansion, every step is measured. The enormity of what I'm about to do looms large, yet there's no turning back. Everything has led to this moment.

I'm flanked by guards almost immediately, their presence as unwelcoming as the cold night air. They're thorough, ensuring I'm not armed, their hands swift and professional as they check for weapons or a wire.

"Just making sure you're not crashing the party with any unwelcome surprises," one mutters, almost humorlessly.

"Appreciate the warm greeting," I reply dryly, unable to resist a comment on the excessive security detail. Their faces remain impassive, no sign they registered my attempt at levity.

Once cleared, I'm ushered inside, another trio of guards taking over to lead me deeper into the mansion. Their silent, imposing forms are a clear message: I'm walking into the lion's den, and they want me to know it.

The journey through the corridors is silent, the tension palpable. We arrive at Aleksey's office, and the door swings open to reveal my half-brother. He stands in front of the window, his silhouette stark against the night sky.

As I step into the room, the door closes behind me with a quiet thud. Aleksey turns, his expression one of cold anticipation, as if he's been waiting for this moment just as much as I have.

"Welcome, brother," he greets, his voice smooth, laced with a venomous charm. "I was beginning to think you wouldn't make it."

I meet his gaze, my resolve steeling within me. "Wouldn't miss it for the world," I respond, stepping further into the room, ready for whatever comes next.

Noticing Nicky skulking to the side, I cut through my half-brother's nonsense and go straight to the point. "Where's Tory? I want to know she's safe." My voice leaves no room for ambiguity; I'm not here to play Aleksey's games.

Aleksey's laugh, sharp and unwelcome, echoes off the walls. "You're in no position to make demands, brother." Despite his words, he signals Nicky with a terse nod. "Go fetch her."

As Nicky exits, Aleksey turns his attention back to me, a smirk playing on his lips. "Playing the hero, huh? You've gone soft, Maksim. You never used to care this much before."

"And you've always lacked the brains for the business, Aleksey. This isn't about being soft. It's about doing what's right, something you wouldn't understand."

The brief flicker of annoyance in Aleksey's eyes tells me my words have hit their mark.

"What happens now?" I demand, every muscle in my body tensed for what comes next.

He leans back, a cold glint in his eye. "You're going to watch as your woman dies, Maksim. And then, it'll be your turn."

I shake my head, incredulous at his shortsightedness. "And you think anyone will follow you after doing something like that? Our father will have you killed for this."

He unfolds his plan with chilling calmness. "Nicky will help me pin it all on one of the guards. Once Father takes care of him, I'll be in line to lead."

I can't help but laugh despite the gravity of our situation. "You sound incredibly stupid, you know that? Every time you open your mouth, it's just astounding." My words are pointed, designed to provoke.

Aleksey's composure cracks, anger flaring in his eyes. "You think you can insult your way out of this?"

"No," I reply, steel in my voice. "I think you're underestimating everyone, especially our father. This plan of yours? It's going to crumble, and I'll be there to see it." My defiance is a clear challenge, throwing his own arrogance back in his face.

Pushing further, I dig into Aleksey's weak spots. "You've always been desperate to prove you're the smartest in the room, brother. But deep down, you know you're not cut out for this. It's not just about sitting in the big chair; it's about earning it, understanding the responsibility. Something you've never quite grasped."

His facade of control begins to crack, his grip tightening around the edge of his desk like a man clinging to the last shreds of his plan.

With a malicious smirk, I continue. "You're a joke, always have been. Too blinded by your own insecurity to see the bigger picture."

Aleksey snaps, the gun in his hand suddenly pointed in my direction. There's a moment where everything seems to hang in the balance, his finger twitching on the trigger. But then, he reins in his rage, holstering the gun with a forced laugh. "You think you're very clever, don't you?"

I find the entire display amusing. "More than you'll ever be," I shoot back.

Our standoff is abruptly interrupted by the door swinging open. Nicky marches in, flanked by guards, with Tory in tow. The sight of her, here, in the flesh and so close yet so far, sends a sharp pain through my chest. Our eyes meet, a silent exchange of worry, relief, and unspoken promises.

We both instinctively move toward each other, only to be held back by the guards. The space between us feels like miles, each second apart an eternity. Despite the grim circumstances, seeing Tory again reignites a flame of hope within me. No matter what Aleksey has planned, we're together now, and that changes everything.

ont2

As Nicky manhandles Tory closer to Aleksey, something inside me snaps. The sight of her in danger, so close to that monster, ignites a fury I can barely contain. Without thinking, I lunge toward them, only to be instantly subdued by the guards, their grips iron-tight, holding me back with force.

Aleksey, seizing the moment, brandishes his gun once again, this time aiming it directly at Tory. His voice is cold, laced with a venomous triumph. "I'm calling the shots now, big brother. If you have any sense left, you'll remember that. Unless you want to die here, start acting like you understand your place."

I'm seething, my response defiant. "You'll kill me regardless. I'm not as stupid as you seem to think." My heart pounds, every instinct screaming to protect Tory, to fight regardless of the odds.

Aleksey gives a nonchalant shrug, his cruelty unwavering. "Maybe I'll just end her life and leave you broken, a constant reminder of what you've lost." His smirk is sinister, enjoying the twisted game he's playing. Then he hints at something more, a deeper layer of his plan. "You don't even grasp the full extent of what's at stake here, Maksim."

Confusion cuts through my anger. "What are you talking about?" I demand, struggling against the guards' hold. My mind races, trying to decipher Aleksey's cryptic taunts. What hasn't he revealed? What more could he possibly have planned?

My brother's silence is maddening, his smile all the more infuriating. He's holding something back, some critical piece of this nightmare I haven't pieced together yet.

. . .

Aleksey's laughter pierces the heavy air, deranged and chilling. "Oh, brother, the look on your face is going to be priceless." He cackles, then drops the bombshell, "Your precious Tory is pregnant."

My world stops. The revelation hits like a physical blow, and for a moment, I'm completely disoriented, the reality of the situation crashing down on me. I turn to Tory, searching her eyes, and find them brimming with tears. The truth in her gaze is undeniable.

Aleksey, reveling in the moment, goads her. "Go on, tell him what you told me." His gun is still menacingly pointed at her.

With a voice barely above a whisper, Tory confirms, "It's true. I'm pregnant." The words hang heavy between us, a revelation that changes everything.

The sight of Aleksey aiming his gun at her, at our unborn child, ignites a rage within me that knows no bounds. In a flash of motion fueled by pure fury, I lash out at the nearest guard, my training taking over. A swift punch to his jaw disorients him enough for me to grab his gun, turning it on Aleksey.

The room is charged with tension, a precarious standoff that could erupt at any second.

"You won't get away with this," I growl, my voice steady despite the turmoil inside me. "Harming Tory, our child... you've crossed a line from which there's no return."

Aleksey, with a twisted grin, doesn't miss a beat. "It's almost pathetic, your misplaced loyalty to someone who means nothing in the grand scheme of things."

I keep my focus, gun steady in my grip even as his words aim to wound. "Is that what you tell yourself to justify this? That everyone else is just collateral damage to your ambition?"

He scoffs, the sound echoing mockingly in the tense air. "Please, you think you're any better? Trying to pretend you're some kind of saint? It's a weak façade, brother. Deep down, you're just as willing to take what's yours by any means necessary."

The distance between Aleksey and me, though not vast, is enough to seed doubt. I'm a good shot, but under these circumstances, with Tory's life hanging in the balance, the margin for error is nonexistent. A miss could seal her fate, and that's a risk I can't take.

And then there's the other plan, the ace up my sleeve I've been anxiously waiting to play. *Where the hell are they?* I wonder, frustration gnawing at me. Timing is everything, and right now, it feels like ours is running out.

Suddenly, the room plunges into darkness.

Aleksey curses loudly, confusion and anger lacing his voice as he demands, "What the fuck is going on?"

A smirk spreads across my face, the first genuine sign of hope since this standoff began. "Looks like our guests have finally arrived," I say, more to myself than anyone else. The cavalry has come, right on cue.

In the cover of darkness, the dynamics shift. This blackout isn't just a power failure; it's a signal, a meticulously planned move announcing the arrival of reinforcements. My heart races, not with fear, but with the adrenaline of impending action.

Aleksey's temporary disorientation gives us a precious advantage. It's time to turn the tables on him, to seize control of the situation and ensure the safety of Tory and our unborn child.

CHAPTER 33

TORY

Like some kind of miracle, everything goes black. It's so dark I can't see my hand in front of my face.

Aleksey's freaking out, his voice cutting through the darkness, "What the fuck is going on?"

Honestly, I'd laugh if the situation weren't so intense.

Seizing the moment, I elbow Aleksey right in the stomach and make a break for it, dashing toward where I last saw Maksim. My heart's pounding so loud, I'm sure it could guide me through this blackout. Just as I'm about to reach him, Aleksey's voice slices through the chaos, ordering his goons to "take us out."

We bolt out of the study with gunshots ringing out behind us. The whole thing feels like a scene from a movie I'd definitely never want to star in. Risking a glance over my shoulder, my eyes have adjusted enough to the darkness to see Nicky still in the room.

Maksim's hand finds mine in the dark, and we're running, dodging a hail of bullets like we're in some kind of high-stakes obstacle course.

We're not exactly out of the woods yet but having Maksim by my side is like a little beacon of hope. Sprinting down Aleksey's fancy hallways, Maksim's holding my hand in one of his, and in the other, he's popping off shots at the guards to keep them at bay.

While we're dodging bullets and making a mad dash for freedom, I ask, "What's with the blackout? Was that part of the plan?" The urgency in my voice probably gives away just how high-strung I am right now.

Maksim barely breaks stride as he answers, "Pulled a few strings," right as the sound of police sirens starts wailing outside.

He tugs me toward the front door, probably thinking we're about to make our grand escape. But nope, the thing won't budge.

"Shit," he hisses. "Security system must be powered by a backup generator."

The place lights up with these creepy red emergency lights. It's like suddenly being in a horror movie, with everything bathed in this unsettling red glow. The shadows look freakier, and the whole vibe just got a lot more sinister.

Stuck in this eerie, red-drenched scene, I catch a glimpse of Maksim's determined face. If there's a way out of this, we'll find it together. His confidence is catching, even now.

We make a beeline for the windows, and through the red haze, I can see the cops swarming outside, weapons at the ready, like they're about to storm a castle. Just as I'm thinking there's a glimmer of hope, massive steel shutters come crashing down, sealing us inside.

"Shit!" Maksim's frustration echoes my own thoughts exactly. He grabs my arm, urgency clear in his voice. "We need to get to the roof."

"Easier said than done!"

Right on cue, a bunch of guards burst into the room like they're the welcoming committee we definitely didn't want. Maksim instantly steps in front of me, shield and defender all in one. He fires off a couple of shots, creating just enough space for us to make a move.

Grabbing my hand, he pulls me toward the stairs. My heart's racing, but Maksim's grip is like a solid promise that he's got me. The sound of guards hot on our heels adds an extra layer of adrenaline to our escape.

Just when I think we're about to be overrun, Maksim does something out of a superhero playbook. With what I swear must be superhuman strength, he shoves a massive armoire down the stairs. It crashes into the pursuing guards like some kind of makeshift bowling game, sending them tumbling.

Watching the madness unfold, I can't help but be a bit awed. Maksim, despite everything, manages to pull off these moments of sheer badassery. As we race up the stairs, leaving the sound of chaos behind, I'm reminded yet again why we're a team not to be messed with.

"What's the plan?" My voice is filled with both fear and adrenaline as we ascend higher.

"We get up as high as we can, then look for a way down from there." Maksim's reply is quick, focused.

At that moment, Aleksey's voice, cold and menacing, filters through the house, promising retribution. "Maksim, I'm coming for you!"

Suddenly, Aleksey himself appears, a dark figure at the end of the hallway, rifle aimed with chilling precision. A shot rings out, and in a breath, Maksim's yanking me aside, the bullet whizzing past where we stood just moments before.

We're running again, up the stairs, the third floor our new destination. The threat of Aleksey and his rifle looms behind us, each step propelled by the desperate need to survive, to find some way out of this madness.

Reaching the top floor feels like a small victory until we see the windows—every single one sealed shut by those merciless steel shutters. All but one. There's a sliver of hope in the form of a window left uncovered, a mistake in Aleksey's fortress. Without hesitation, Maksim takes aim and fires, shattering the glass into a thousand pieces of liberation.

He turns to me, urgency written all over his face. "You first," he says, guiding me toward the window. Climbing out onto the roof, the night air hits me, fear and relief swirling inside. I look down, and it's a long way to the ground. Cops swarm below, a beacon of safety just out of reach.

Aleksey's voice echoes up to us, filled with rage, followed by more gunshots trying to find their mark. I hold my breath as Maksim makes his climb, and then we're both on the roof, a pair of fugitives perched on high.

Above us, the sound of salvation—choppy and loud. A helicopter hovers, a beacon in the night, and the realization hits me like a lightning bolt. That's our way out, our escape from this nightmare.

Maksim catches my gaze, a shared understanding passing between us. We don't have to say it; we're thinking the same thing. It's risky, insane even, but it beats the alternative of facing Aleksey's wrath head-on.

With the helicopter in sight, hope surges anew. It's a wild, desperate plan, but then again, hasn't this whole night been made of those? Now, we just have to make it aboard.

Maksim is furiously signaling to the helicopter, which, miraculously, starts to descend toward us. Just as it feels like we're moments away from a breathtaking escape, Aleksey bursts onto the roof, his timing impeccable, his aim deadly. He fires off a shot, and the helicopter, reacting to the immediate danger, pulls away, ascending back into the night sky.

Aleksey marches toward us with his gun ready, hurling insults and bitter truths our way. "You've always been the favorite, Maksim! I was never given a chance to prove myself!" His voice is full of resentment and rage, a lifetime of living in the shadow of his half-brother boiling over.

Maksim steps in front of me, a human barrier against Aleksey's wrath. He warns me, a grim sort of calm in his voice, "He's more likely to hit us with that rifle than for me to hit him with the pistol."

It's clear – Aleksey has the advantage, and on the rooftop there's nowhere to hide.

Tension crackles in the air, a tangible force as both men raise their weapons, a silent declaration that this could end in bloodshed. My heart's racing, every beat a prayer for a miracle, for a way out of this madness.

As if my prayers are answered, Nicky appears, a shadow turned savior. The sight of him, gun raised and aimed at Aleksey, is so unexpected it's almost surreal. But the real shock comes when he reveals a badge—Nicky's a cop?

"Put the gun down, Aleksey. Now," he commands, his voice leaving no room for argument.

The revelation sends shockwaves through me.

Aleksey, looking like he's just lost the only game he's ever cared about, finally drops his gun. It's like someone hit the pause button on him. Meanwhile, our ride out of this mess decides it's showtime again, dropping a ladder down to us. Maksim insists I go first. Climbing up that ladder, I can't help but take a last look at the chaos we're leaving behind. The house, the swarming cops—it's a madhouse.

Once I'm safely inside, and Maksim follows, he slips into what I can only describe as boss mode. He starts barking orders like he's been doing this kind of dramatic escape his whole life.

"To the hospital," he says, all business, making sure I'm okay. And just like that, we're flying off into the night, the mansion and all its nightmares shrinking into the distance.

Maksim pulls me close, and I've gotta say, after a night like this, being in his arms is exactly where I want to be. It's been a rollercoaster, but with him by my side, I feel like we can handle whatever comes next. Plus, hospital or not, we're together, and right now, that's all that matters.

While we're flying to safety, Maksim starts spilling the beans on the whole operation. Turns out, he's got a few buddies in the Chicago PD, guys who don't mind bending the rules for the right price. The original plan? Have a few cop cars roll up to Aleksey's place, put on a bit of a show to spook him into letting me go. Maksim's not one for showing his hand unless he absolutely has to. But me being in danger? That changed the game entirely.

But he looks genuinely puzzled.

What showed up... that was way more than a couple of cop cars. I wasn't expecting a helicopter. These are the Feds."

I can't help but chuckle, despite the craziness of it all. "So you didn't order the dramatic rescue?" I ask, half-teasing, half-amazed at the turn of events.

Maksim just shakes his head, a small smile playing on his lips. He's got that look where he's trying to piece together a puzzle with half the pieces missing.

The moment we get to the hospital, Maksim switches into full-on protector mode, his focus laser-sharp on getting me seen by a doctor ASAP.

"Really, Maksim, I'm okay," I try to reassure him, attempting to slow his determined march to the emergency room.

But he's having none of it. With a determined look in his eye, he retorts, "Not a chance. We're not taking any risks with you or our little one. You're getting checked out, end of story."

I smile, despite the situation. His unwavering commitment to our well-being, this fierce protectiveness, it's both comforting and a tad overwhelming. "Okay, okay, Mr. Over-protective," I concede, playfully rolling my eyes. "Lead the way."

He glances back at me, a mix of concern and love softening his features. "Just doing my job. Keeping my favorite girls safe."

Girls? I grin, imagining he has some magical ability to know the sex of the little one inside me.

I'm whisked off to an examination room, and Maksim's right there, sticking close. When I grab his hand, look him in the eye, and assure him I'm really fine, he eases up a bit.

The doc finally gives me the all-clear, and I can't help but feel a bit amused. I was half expecting Maksim to flip if there was even a hint of bad news. But all's well, and seeing Maksim try to dial back his inner protector – just barely – is kind of funny, actually.

Right when I'm starting to really enjoy the calm after the storm, there's a knock at the door. Igor walks in, and you can almost see the tension melt off him when he sees we're both alright.

"Adelina and Irina are on their way," he says. "They're safe." He turns to me and says, "Well, you've certainly had a memorable introduction into our world."

I smile at him. "Most fun I've had in years." That earns a chuckle from him. It's weirdly nice, finding humor after a night like we've had.

As Igor's gaze settles on Maksim, there's a gravity in his demeanor that wasn't there before. "I'm disappointed in Aleksey," he begins, his voice heavy with regret. "But he chose his path." He pauses, and there's a hint of introspection that suggests this situation has hit closer to home than he'd like to admit.

"This whole ordeal has been a wake-up call for me," Igor continues, a thoughtful frown creasing his brow. "I wasn't as attuned to the growing rift in our family as I should have been. Perhaps I'm more ready for retirement than I thought."

It's a moment of vulnerability from a man who has been in control for a long time, and it doesn't go unnoticed. Maksim, with his unshakable composure, responds with a nod, his face an open book of readiness to take on whatever comes next. "I'm ready, whenever you decide it's time," he assures his father, his voice firm and full of the resolve that's gotten us through the night.

The air in the room shifts slightly, filled with the unspoken understanding that transitions are on the horizon—not just for Igor and Maksim, but for all of us.

Sitting there, witnessing this exchange, I feel a surge of respect for both men. They're facing the aftermath of a crisis not just with resilience, but with a forward-looking gaze, ready to embrace whatever changes lie ahead.

Igor's mood lightens, a smile breaking through the somber atmosphere as he looks at us. "You two deserve some rest, a bit of peace after everything you've been through," he says, the warmth in his voice a balm.

Maksim reaches out, placing a reassuring hand on his father's shoulder. "We'd love to have you over this weekend. It'd be good for all of us," he suggests, the invitation genuine and open.

Igor nods, his expression softening further. "I'd like that," he agrees, a sense of relief in his acceptance. With one final smile of gratitude and affection, he makes his way out, leaving us to process the whirlwind of events that have brought us to this moment.

The road ahead will clearly be filled with its own set of challenges, particularly for Igor. But there's a sense of unity, a strength in the promise of facing them together.

With Igor gone, the room feels a whole lot quieter, a private bubble in the midst of the hospital's ceaseless hum. Maksim looks at me, his face etching into something serious, and my heart kicks up a notch. Is another storm coming?

I dive right in, overflowing with gratitude. "Maksim, I can't even start to thank you enough for everything you did tonight, for saving me." I mean every word, feeling both awe and deep appreciation for this man who's turned my world upside down in the best way possible. "I shou—"

He cuts me off with a simple, "No." That's it. Just "no." And I'm sitting here, totally befuddled.

He moves closer, perches on the edge of the bed, and takes my hand in his. The serious vibe doesn't budge, and if anything, it deepens. "No, I'm the one who should be thanking you," he insists, and I'm not sure where he's going with this. "You've opened my heart in ways I didn't even know were closed. You reminded me there's so much more to life than this endless cycle of scheming and crime.

"And... thank you for the gift of carrying our child," he says, and there's a shimmer in his eyes, like he's on the verge of tears. But just as quick as I think I see it, it's gone, like a raindrop evaporating in the sun.

"And, I need to apologize."

I squeeze his hand, trying to convey a world of support and confusion in one gesture. "Maksim, apologize for what? After everything tonight, I can't imagine..."

He looks away for a moment, collecting his thoughts, then locks his gaze back on mine. His voice drops. "I need to apologize for being a coward," he starts, and a bubble of laughter threatens to escape. The idea of him, of all people, being a coward just doesn't add up.

But he's serious, his gaze steady. "I've been hiding my feelings, Tory. Carrying this love for you in my heart, but too afraid to let it out. I've been a coward in that sense."

His confession stops me cold, laughter dying on my lips.

"I can't hide it anymore. I love you, Tory. Truly, deeply, endlessly. And I want to spend my life protecting you, being with you if that's what you want."

The room feels charged, filled with the gravity of his words, his offer hanging between us like a lifeline.

"But if you don't want this, if you don't want the danger and the complications that come with my world, I'll understand. I'll step back, and I won't trouble you with it again," he finishes, his voice barely above a whisper, leaving the choice entirely in my hands.

How do you even respond to an offer like that? To a declaration so raw and earnest? It's overwhelming, the depth of his love, the sincerity in his offer to either dive into this life together or to let me go for my own peace.

I reach for his hand, entwining our fingers together, the gesture simple but filled with my own unsaid feelings. "Maksim," I say, my voice steady, "I don't want an out. I want this life, as complicated and dangerous as it may be, but only if it's with you.

"I love you too, Maksim," I whisper, the words feeling like they're sealing some sacred vow between us. We lean in for a hug, a perfect movie moment, until I let out a sudden "Ow!"

"What? What's wrong?" he asks, looking at me.

"Apparently, I'm a bit more banged up than I realized."

Maksim's concern is etched in every line of his face. "Maybe we should stay a bit longer in the hospital," he suggests, always the protector.

"Hell no," I answer immediately. "The idea of spending one more minute in this hospital room is about as appealing as a root canal without anesthetic."

248 | K.C. CROWNE

He chuckles, the sound warm in the sterile room. Then he gets serious again, but there's a twinkle in his eye. "And if you even think about joking that you're going back to your office and that damn Murphy bed, you've got another think coming."

A surprised laugh escapes my lips, remembering all the times that Murphy bed had been the center of our little adventures. "Hey, I've got some pretty good memories of that Murphy bed," I retort playfully. "Thanks to you."

His voice is soft but firm when he says, "I want you to come home with me, Tory. To live with Adelina and me."

The words wash over me like a balm, soothing away the last of my doubts. His offer is everything I didn't know I needed to hear. Smiling, I look into his eyes, seeing our future reflected back at me. "I'd like that," I say, my heart full. "I'd like that very much."

And just like that, in a hospital room that's seen more than its fair share of pain and heartache, we find a moment of perfect happiness.

CHAPTER 35

W e don't hang around the hospital longer than we have to. As we're going through the motions of checking out, my phone buzzes with a message from Irina, saying they're almost at the hospital. The thought of finally heading home, of being away from all this chaos, feels like a breath of fresh air.

Tory's making small talk with the staff in the lobby. Her resilience amazes me—after everything, she still has the strength to smile, to be kind. It's one of the many things I admire about her.

I turn my head and see FBI agents milling about the lobby. Their presence throws me for a loop. As I explained to Tory, my plan was simple: a bit of intimidation courtesy of the local police to rattle Aleksey. Yet the FBI is now involved, their interest in Aleksey's apprehension a clear indicator that this went way beyond my expectations.

And the way they're glancing over at me, with measured, assessing looks, is unnerving. It sparks a flicker of doubt, the kind that whispers maybe I'm not just a bystander in their eyes. Could they be here for me as well?

The gravity of the situation weighs on me. This isn't just about Aleksey's downfall anymore; it's about the aftermath, about how deep the repercussions might go. As Tory finishes up and turns back to me, her smile a sharp contrast to the churning of my thoughts, I'm reminded of what's at stake. Our future, our safety, our family—it's all on the line.

Pushing those thoughts aside, I focus on the immediate: getting us out of here, back to the safety and normalcy of home. As we weave through the lobby, trying to maintain a sense of normalcy despite the heavy FBI presence, Tory leans in, curiosity in her voice. "What are they doing here?"

"I'm not exactly sure," I admit quietly.

The truth is, the sight of them has put me on edge. There's a charged moment where it feels like they might zero in on us, but then, nothing. We pass by without incident, leaving me to puzzle over their intentions. Was this meant to be a show of force, a subtle warning perhaps?

The realization that I might have some local PD in my corner but stand on shaky ground with the Feds is unsettling. Father has always drilled into me the importance of keeping a clean record, of steering clear of anything that might draw federal attention. His teachings are the only reason I can walk out of here without cuffs around my wrists.

Stepping out into the cool evening, the relief of being free from the hospital and the probing eyes of the FBI is palpable. Tory and I are just starting to relax when a familiar voice stops us in our tracks.

"Hell of a night, huh?"

As the shadowy figure steps forward, the adrenaline that had just started to ebb away comes surging back. It's Nicky. Instinctively, I position myself between him and Tory, wary of any more surprises this night might throw our way.

"We've had enough trouble for one day," I say, a clear warning in my voice.

Nicky, hands raised, offers a small smile. "I come in peace," he assures us. His slight Russian accent colors his words.

"Is that so?" I challenge, not ready to drop my defenses just yet. The night has been too full of surprises for me to take anything at face value.

"Yeah, believe it or not," Nicky says, his voice getting a touch more serious. "I'm with the FBI. Been undercover for a good while, keeping an eye on Aleksey's schemes."

I can't hide my disbelief. "Is that right?" The words slip out, tinged with skepticism. The thought of Nicky being on the side of the law is a lot to wrap my head around.

He nods, confirming my suspicion. "While you and Igor have managed to keep your activities clean—at least, on paper—Aleksey hasn't been quite as cautious with his endeavors. He caught our attention, and I was assigned to go undercover, gain entry into his inner circle."

The news isn't exactly a shock. Aleksey's recklessness has always set him apart from mine and my father's more calcu-lated approach to our world. Nicky's presence here, now, could mean a number of things for our future. But for the moment, it seems we're on the right side of the law, a small comfort after a night filled with too many close calls.

Tory, not one to stay silent, pipes up with a glare. "I don't care who you are or who you're with. You hit me." Her voice carries anger and defiance, making it clear she's not easily swayed by badges or titles.

Nicky has the grace to look genuinely remorseful. "I'm truly sorry for that. I had to keep up appearances, play the part. But, for what it's worth, you got a couple good shots in too. Nearly broke my arm with that pool cue."

A smirk plays on Tory's lips, a flash of satisfaction at his admission. "You deserved it," she retorts, her tone light but pointed.

Turning back to the matter at hand, I press him for more information. "Why are you here? What do you want from us?"

Nicky takes a deep breath before answering, the weight of his undercover life apparent. "Even after spending a year close to Aleksey, the only solid charge we've got on him is the aggravated kidnapping of Tory. Turns out, he didn't trust me as much as I thought."

The irony of the situation isn't lost on us. Aleksey's mistrust, his paranoia about loyalty, might have just been his undoing.

Nicky, maintaining a professional demeanor, shifts the conversation toward me. "I came to give you the lowdown, Maksim. We know you're poised to become the biggest name in Chicago's underworld once your father steps down. But you should know, you're not on our radar."

Tory looks puzzled at this. "I don't get it. Why tell us this?"

Nicky sighs, sounding a bit worn. "It's about choosing the lesser of two evils, really. Say we busted you, created a power vacuum. What fills it might be worse."

He then fixes his gaze on me. "Just a heads-up, though. Keep things clean. If you cross the line, our next meeting won't be as cordial."

Just as we're wrapping up our conversation, headlights slice through the darkness—a welcome interruption. It's Irina's car, and my heart does a little leap at the thought of seeing Adelina.

Nicky catches the change in atmosphere and decides it's his time to bow out. "Guess that's my signal," he murmurs before slipping away as quietly as he came.

The moment the car door swings open, Adelina's out and into my arms like a shot. "Papa!" she exclaims, wrapping her little arms around me as tightly as she can. I hug her back, feeling the weight of the world melt away in her embrace. It's one of those moments, so full of love and relief, that you wish you could freeze in time.

Soon after, we're all settled in the car, Irina taking the driver's seat like she's piloting us back to normalcy. Tory leans against me, her warmth a comforting presence, and Adelina, ever the daddy's girl, rests her head on my shoulder. As we pull away, I reflect on the life I've chosen, the dangers and the unpredictability of that life.

But in moments like this, surrounded by the people I love, I'm reminded why it's worth it. Life in the Bratva is a roller-coaster, but these moments of peace, of simple human connection, they're what keep me grounded. They're a reminder to savor every second of love and calm.

I vow to treasure every one of them.

EPILOGUE I

MAKSIM

Seven months later...

"I can't believe I let you two talk me into this," I grumble, looking down at Howard the Great Dane currently enjoying a bath more than I am. My arms are covered in suds, and Howard, oblivious to the chaos he's caused, wags his tail, splashing soapy water everywhere.

Tory with her big, rounded belly, sidles up next to me, her warmth a stark contrast to the cold water. "Thank you," she says, pressing a quick kiss to my cheek. "There's no way I could have managed this."

I can't help but soften at her gratitude, despite the mess. "Yeah, well," I start, trying to maintain my gruff demeanor, "next time, Ty and Cassie better keep a closer eye on him. Speaking of which..." My voice trails off, expecting to see Ty skulking around, avoiding the chaos.

From across the room, Ty's voice carries over, laced with humor. "I'm on poop patrol over here! You think this is a

256 of K.C. Crowne

walk in the park?" His laughter echoes, and I shake my head, unable to suppress my own chuckle.

Adelina, ever eager to be involved, claps her hands in delight at the sight of Howard enjoying his bath. "Papa, Howard looks so happy!" she exclaims, her enthusiasm infectious.

Looking around at the makeshift family we've formed, here in this moment of domestic chaos at the doggie daycare, I realize there's nowhere else I'd rather be. The life I lead feels miles away when I'm here with them, elbow deep in soapy water, surrounded by laughter and love.

The day's work might be unconventional for a man of my background, but in this life we're building, every moment is a gift—even the messy ones.

I finally manage to hoist Howard out of the tub. The moment he's free, he starts shaking, sending a fresh wave of water all over us. "Ah, come on, Howard!" I laugh, even as I'm drenched yet again.

Adelina's squeals of delight fill the room as she chases after Howard, towel in hand. "Papa, look! I'm gonna get him dry!" she declares, her determination as strong as her laughter.

Howard, thrilled with this new game, bounds around with the energy only a Great Dane can muster. "He thinks you're playing chase, Ade!" I call out, watching the joyous chaos unfold.

Adelina, undeterred, giggles and darts after Howard, who's more than happy to keep the game going. Watching them, a laugh escapes me, and I realize this wet, laughter-filled moment is perfect.

"You're gonna need a bigger towel!" I tease.

By the time we're wrapping up for the day, Adelina and I are both beat. The doggie daycare has a way of draining every ounce of energy you thought you had, and then some. Ty and Cassie shout their goodbyes as we head toward the door, the familiar sounds of the daycare fading behind us.

Tory locks the front door, turning to us with a smile. "Ready to head home?" she asks, a tired but content note in her voice. She pauses, her hand flying to her belly. Her eyes go wide as she looks over at me, a mix of surprise and urgency clear as day. "I think it's time."

I freeze, caught completely off guard. "Is that the first contraction?" I ask, trying to keep my voice steady.

She shakes her head, her expression serious. "No, but this is the one that tells me it's really happening."

For a moment, my exhaustion vanishes, replaced by a jolt of adrenaline. And then there's Adelina, her excitement palpable, her scream of joy filling the air. "I'm going to have a little sister!" Her enthusiasm is infectious, her joy a bright spot in the sudden rush of the moment.

The reality of the situation hits me full force—we're about to welcome another member into our family. Every worry, every bit of tiredness, fades into the background. This is it, the moment we've been preparing for, and all I can think about is Tory and our soon-to-be-born daughter.

As we all scramble into the car, Adelina immediately charmingly takes charge. "Okay, remember. Inhale, one, two, three... and exhale," she instructs with an earnest focus that would be comical if it weren't so incredibly sweet.

From the driver's seat, I steal glances in the rearview mirror, watching this beautiful scene unfold. Tory plays along, following Adelina's instructions with a smile. "Like this, Ade?" Tory asks, her voice full of amusement and love.

"That's right! You got it!" Adelina encourages, her role as the big sister already in full swing. My heart couldn't possibly be fuller; the love and connection flowing through our car feels like a tangible force.

When we reach the hospital, the urgency of the situation kicks my instincts into overdrive. I rush to grab a wheelchair, brushing aside Tory's attempts to downplay the drama. "No arguments, love. We're doing this right," I assert, my voice leaving no room for debate as I help her into the chair with all the care in the world.

Tory looks up at me, a soft smile playing on her lips, understanding and trust in her eyes. "Okay, okay, you win. Lead the way, my knight in shining armor," she teases gently.

"Ready for this?" I whisper as we approach the reception desk, squeezing her hand for reassurance.

With a nod and a smile that lights up her face, she replies, "With you? Always."

In the midst of the anticipation, I take a moment to share our joy with those who matter most. Sending a quick text to my father and Tiffany, I can almost feel their excitement through the phone.

Soon, Tory is settled into a maternity room, the air buzzing with a mixture of nerves and excitement. The process of bringing new life into the world is both miraculous and daunting. As the medical team moves efficiently, preparing

Tory, I find myself caught between wanting to be her pillar of strength and feeling an overwhelming sense of awe.

I hold Tory's hand, offering words of encouragement and love. Each contraction she faces, each moment of discomfort, I feel it alongside her, wishing I could bear some of the burden. Yet, through it all, her strength amazes me—her resilience and grace under pressure, qualities that made me fall in love with her, shine brighter than ever.

And then, hours later, the moment arrives—the room fills with the first cries of our newborn. It's a sound that cuts through all the tension, transforming it into pure, unadulterated joy. Watching as the doctors carefully clean and swaddle our baby before placing her in Tory's arms is a moment so raw and beautiful, it imprints itself on my heart. Stealing glance after glance at our baby girl, I find myself caught in a loop of disbelief and wonder. She's impossibly small, impossibly perfect. Every little feature, from the delicate curve of her cheek to the tiny fingers curled into fists, feels like a miracle I can't quite wrap my head around.

Tory, with our daughter in her arms, looks every bit the natural mother I knew she would be. There's a grace and ease to her actions, a tender, unwavering love in her gaze that fills the room with warmth. Watching them together, I'm struck by a profound sense of completeness, a feeling that everything in my life has led to this moment.

Eventually, it's time for me to take our daughter into my arms, the weight of her tiny body against my chest both terrifying and exhilarating. Holding her close, feeling the gentle rhythm of her breath, my heart swells to the point of aching. It's a love so intense, so all-consuming, it borders on the indescribable.

In that moment, surrounded by the quiet sounds of the maternity ward, a name comes to me—a Russian one, one that feels like it carries the weight of our hopes and dreams for her.

"What about Kira?" I whisper, the name feeling right as it leaves my lips.

Tory, her eyes shining with tears and joy, nods. "It's perfect," she agrees, her voice soft but sure.

Leaning down, I press a kiss to Kira's forehead, a promise of protection and love sealed with the simplest of gestures. Turning to Tory, I kiss her too.

Just as we're settling into this new reality, the door swings open and in bounces Adelina, my father trailing behind her. I'm taken aback, having expected my father to arrive later, but there he is, wearing a broad grin.

Father chuckles at my obvious surprise. "You think I'd miss the birth of my granddaughter?" he asks, amusement dancing in his eyes. "Maksim, my boy, if you thought that, maybe you're the one who's lost his marbles."

The room fills with a warm laughter at his jest, and with a heart swelling with pride, I carefully pass Kira into my father's arms. Watching him, I'm reminded of the first time he held Adelina—there's a gentleness in him, a tenderness I've only ever seen in moments like these.

Father, with Kira cradled expertly in his arms, seems to embody a quiet strength and love. It's a sight that ties together past and present, a reminder of the enduring bonds of family. After a moment that feels both fleeting and eternal, he gently hands Kira to Tory, his eyes soft with affection.

Adelina, ever eager, moves closer, her fascination and love for her new sister evident in every word and gesture. "She's so tiny," she whispers, her voice filled with awe and a hint of the protective sister she's sure to become.

The room feels like a sanctuary, a place where love and family intertwine to create something truly magical. As Tory and Adelina coo over Kira, Father beckons me to a quieter corner of the room.

"First off," he starts, glancing at Tory and the baby with a smile, "Tiffany wanted to be here, but she's visiting Aleksey. Trying to make sense of everything."

I nod, understanding the complexity of their situation. "How's she handling everything?" I ask, genuinely concerned for both of them.

Father sighs, a heavy sound. "Still processing. It's a lot for a mother to deal with."

The conversation shifts, his gaze meeting mine squarely. "I've been doing some thinking," he says, his voice taking on a solemn note. "I'll handle matters, sort things out, prepare the Bratva for the transfer. And when you're ready, I'll hand over the reins to you."

The honor and responsibility of his trust in me feels immense. "I'm humbled, Father," I reply, the significance of his decision not lost on me.

He chuckles, a sound that fills the room with a lighter energy. "Don't let it go to your head, son. You're not in charge yet."

His eyes then drift back to Kira, a softness in his expression I've seen only a few times. "Seeing this little one... It's made me realize it's time for me to focus on being a grandfather."

He turns back to me, a proud smile spreading across his face. "Congratulations, Maksim. You're going to make a fine leader."

Father gives me a firm clap on the shoulder, pulling me back from the future's looming responsibilities. "Now's not the time for shop talk," he says with a chuckle that rumbles deep from his chest. "We'll have plenty of time for that. Right now, I've got another granddaughter to start doting on."

He's right. This moment isn't about transitions of power or the future of the Bratva. It's about family, about the tiny, new life that's brought us all together under such extraordinary circumstances.

We all gather around Tory and Kira again, the room instantly warming with laughter, soft coos, and the kind of love that fills every corner, pushing out the shadows of our past and present concerns. Watching Adelina gently touch Kira's hand, seeing Father's eyes soften as he watches his granddaughters, and feeling Tory lean into me, her strength and warmth melding into mine—I'm overwhelmed by a sense of peace, of contentment.

It's a feeling so rare and precious, especially in our tumultuous world, that I commit every detail to memory. The weight of Kira in my arms earlier, the sound of Adelina's laughter, the way Tory's eyes meet mine with a love so profound it anchors me—this is what it's all about. This is the life I'm fighting for, the future I'll shape not just for me, but for all of us.

In this room, with my family gathered around, I'm reminded that no matter what challenges lie ahead, we have each other. And with that knowledge, I feel a strength and a resolve settle deep within me, ready for whatever comes our way, knowing we'll face it together, as a family.

EPILOGUE II

TORY

Three years later…

Settled in my home office, the laptop screen flickers with the faces of Ty, Cassie, and a few other key members of our Paws and Play team. I lean in, feeling every bit the boss lady as we dive into our mid-year review, dissecting the progress and challenges of our three locations.

"Okay, team, let's talk numbers and narratives," I begin, flipping through the tabs on my screen to pull up our performance metrics. "We've seen impressive growth in our Lincoln Park and Wicker Park spots, but I think it's time we consider expanding further north, maybe into Rogers Park. Thoughts?"

Ty jumps in, his humor never far behind. "As long as we don't start offering cat yoga, I'm in. I can't handle any more 'purrrfect balance' puns, Tory."

Cassie rolls her eyes but smiles. "I think it's a great idea, Tory. There's a real demand up north. But are we stretching too thin, too fast?"

The screen lights up with nods and thoughtful expressions, everyone considering the balance between growth and sustainability.

"I want us to mull it over for the rest of the year," I say, determined to make a calculated move rather than a rushed decision. "No cat yoga, Ty, I promise. But maybe doga?"

Ty's laugh is infectious, even through the digital divide. "Doga? Dogs doing yoga? Now, that I've got to see. Count me in for the demonstration."

The back-and-forth continues, ideas bouncing around, the team's dynamics vibrant and full of potential. We discuss staffing needs, potential locations, and marketing strategies, all while Ty's sass keeps the mood light and engaging.

As the call winds down, I feel a rush of gratitude for this team, for their dedication and spirit. "Thanks, everyone. Your hard work and creativity are what make Paws and Play such a success. Let's keep pushing, keep innovating, and we'll make this expansion a reality."

Closing the laptop, I lean back in my chair, a sense of contentment washing over me. This business, our team, it's more than just a job—it's a passion, a community. And as I gaze out the window, thinking about the future of Paws and Play, I'm filled with excitement for what's to come.

The tranquility of our garden stretches out before me and a moment of reflection washes over. It's almost surreal, this life I'm living now. Paws and Play is thriving beyond my wildest dreams, a testament to the hard work, love, and maybe a bit of luck we've poured into it.

I've reached a point where I've been able to delegate the bulk of the daily operations to Ty and our incredible team of managers. They're the backbone of our success, allowing me the space to still be involved without being over-whelmed by the minutiae.

Each day, I make it a point to visit our shops, not just to ensure things are running smoothly, but also because Adelina and Kira have fallen in love with the pups. Their laughter and joy when we're there, amidst the wagging tails and playful barks, remind me why I started the business in the first place.

Stepping back from the day-to-day grind has also opened up a new world for me—one where family takes center stage. The ability to spend quality time with Maksim, Adelina, and little Kira is something I cherish deeply. Watching Kira grow, seeing her and Adelina play in the garden, and sharing quiet moments with Maksim are the highlights of my day. This balance between passion for my work and love for my family is more fulfilling than I could have ever imagined.

As I pull away from the window, a smile finds its way onto my face. This life, with its blend of business success and family bliss, is more than I ever hoped for. I'm grateful for every chaotic, messy, beautiful moment of it. It's a reminder that dreams don't have to be just dreams—they can be your reality, if you're willing to chase them with all your heart.

The sound of laughter, pure and joyful, draws me away from my reflections and down the stairs, curiosity and a familiar warmth guiding my steps. In the heart of our home, is a scene that captures the essence of happiness: Adelina and Kira, engrossed in the simple pleasure of building a tower with blocks. Their concentration and teamwork, punctuated by bursts of giggles, fill the room with life.

Maksim is there too, a gentle giant among his girls, throwing in his playful suggestions that spark more laughter. Watching him with our daughters, so involved and loving, reinforces everything I feel about this man, about our family.

I am mesmerized by Kira, watching her little hands pick up blocks with determination. She's growing so fast, each day bringing new discoveries, new joys. The love I have for these girls is overwhelming, grounding, and exhilarating all at once. Being a mom has unlocked a part of my heart I didn't even know existed, and every moment with Kira and Adelina feels like a gift.

Catching Maksim's eye, we share a look that says everything without words. It's a shared understanding, a mutual gratitude for this life we're building, for the love that surrounds us. Standing there, watching our girls play, I'm struck by the sheer rightness of it all, by the sense of belonging and purpose that fills me.

As Maksim effortlessly closes the distance between us, his arm finds its familiar place around my waist, pulling me in for a kiss that still manages to make my heart flutter, despite the playful interruption from Adelina.

"Ew, gross," she protests, but her voice is full of mirth, joining in our laughter.

Breaking away, Maksim shares his plans for the evening. "It's date night," he announces with that look in his eyes that promises more than just dinner and a movie. "Father and Tiffany will be here soon to watch the girls."

His hand sneaks a playful squeeze, and I can't help but smile at the insinuation. The conversation shifts as I remember a piece of gossip that's been circulating. "Speaking of Tiffany, is it true? She and Igor are trying for another baby?"

Maksim nods, a mix of pride and confidentiality in his expression. "Trying? You should see the bill for the IVF treatments. It was a success last month." The joy in his voice is unmistakable.

My reaction must have been more visible than I thought because Maksim quickly hushes me with a finger to his lips. "They'll be sharing the news soon," he whispers, a shared secret between us now.

The room feels charged with the excitement of our little secret and the anticipation of our evening together. Diving back into the whirlwind of playtime, my thoughts begin to wander, but this time with a lighter touch. Maksim, who's been steering the Bratva ship with the same kind of 'involved yet hands-off' style I've adopted with Paws and Play, has truly come into his own.

The Bratva under his command has grown into the city's powerhouse, so much so that it's become a bit of a no-brainer that no one dares to rock the boat—though, of course, there have been a few bold souls who've tried.

The saga with Aleksey feels like it's from another lifetime now. His stint with the law has him tucked away for a good long stretch, which, in a way, has closed a turbulent chapter for us, letting us breathe a little easier.

And Tiffany, she's been nothing short of amazing. It's pretty clear she's made her peace with the rollercoaster life that comes with our men. The way she's been with me—no grudges, just open arms—really makes me feel lucky. It's like we've got this unspoken bond, understanding the craziness we're tied to without having to say a word.

Caught up in these musings while watching Maksim play with Adelina and Kira, I'm struck by how we've managed to blend our not-so-ordinary life with moments of pure, simple joy. Here we are, in the midst of our unique chaos, finding our slice of happiness, building a life that's as full of love and laughter as it is complex.

Watching the girls giggle as Maksim pretends to be a monster chasing them around, I feel a wave of affection for this life we've built. Sure, it's a bit unconventional, maybe even a tad perilous, but it's ours.

The moment Igor and Tiffany walk through the door, the atmosphere shifts to one of pure delight. Adelina and Kira's excitement is palpable, their cries of *"Dedushka!"* and *"Babushka!"* filling the room with warmth and joy. Kira, primarily an English speaker, manages the Russian titles with an adorable accent that never fails to make everyone smile.

With the girls happily preoccupied with their grandparents, Maksim and I slip out for our much-anticipated date night. Maksim, in his suit, manages to look effortlessly handsome, causing my heart to skip a beat or two every time I glance his way.

Our evening unfolds with the perfect blend of romance and fun. Dinner is a cozy affair, filled with intimate conversations and shared laughter, a testament to the deep connection we've nurtured over time. Afterwards, we find ourselves lost in the rhythm of the dance floor, moving together as if we're the only ones in the world. The music, the lights, the ambiance—it all blends into a perfect backdrop for a night dedicated to us, to our love.

After our perfect evening out, we find ourselves back at home, quickly slipping into the comfortable and familiar sanctuary of our room. Despite the years together, our kisses still hold the electric charge of new love.

As we kiss and slip out of our clothes, the world outside fades away, leaving just the two of us. Our kisses, deep and full of years of love, spark that familiar fire, each one a reminder of our journey together, of every challenge faced and joy shared.

"It's amazing... seems like every kiss is like the first time," Maksim murmurs against my lips, his hands tracing the contours of my back, pulling me closer.

I laugh softly, the sound mingling with the quiet ambiance of our room. "Is that your way of saying you're still madly in love with me, Mr. Morozov?"

"Madly doesn't even begin to cover it," he replies, his eyes locking onto mine with an intensity that sends my heart racing. It's in these moments, in the simplicity of our love, that I find the greatest joy.

He leads me to the bed, our steps synchronized, a dance we've mastered over the years. Together, under the sheets, we take our time with one another, touching and teasing and loving, bringing each other to climax in each other's arms.

Later, nestled together in the serene quiet that follows, our conversation takes a playful turn, the ease between us a testament to the years we've shared.

"You know," Maksim starts, a mischievous twinkle in his eye, "I think I might have finally perfected my dance moves tonight."

I chuckle, nudging him gently. "Oh, is that right? I guess all those lessons are finally paying off. You might just be ready for the big leagues."

He laughs, pulling me closer. "As long as I have you as my dance partner, I'm ready for anything." Then a thoughtful expression forms on his face.

"Something on your mind, babe?" I ask. Part of me is worried he has bad news to share – always a risk in his line of work.

The light in his eyes grows softer, more earnest. "There's something I've been wanting to share with you."

Curiosity piqued, I watch as he reaches toward the nightstand, pulling open the drawer. There's a moment of suspense, a breath held between us, before he turns back to me, holding a small, velvet box.

My heart skips a beat, my breath catches in my throat. He opens the box to reveal a ring, stunning in its simplicity and beauty. The world seems to stand still.

"Maksim..." I start, but words fail me, emotions swirling too fast to catch.

He smiles the smile that's seen me through my highest highs and my lowest lows.

"Tory," he begins, his voice steady, "from the moment we met, you've captivated me, challenged me, and made me a better man. Every day with you is a gift, a new adventure I want to embark on for the rest of my life. I love you more than words can express, and I can't imagine my world without you in it. Will you marry me?"

Tears of joy blur my vision as his words wash over me, each one a testament to our journey, our love. The room spins, filled with the enormity of this moment, of his question.

"Yes," I breathe out, the word a declaration, a promise. "Yes, I will!"

Ecstatic, he slips the ring onto my finger, a perfect fit, a symbol of our bond, our future. We embrace, laughter and my tears mingling in a beautiful cacophony of emotions. In his arms, I find my home, my future, my forever.

The warmth of his embrace, the sound of his laughter, it's all I need to feel at peace. Yet as I start to drift off to sleep, nestled in his arms, a thought nudges at the edge of my consciousness—a new, life-changing secret *I've* been holding onto. The positive pregnancy test hidden away in the night-stand drawer, a promise of a new chapter waiting to unfold.

I decide to spill the beans about the baby tomorrow. I can't help but grin like a madwoman. My heart's so full it could burst. Imagining the look on Maksim's face, and then getting to tell everyone else? It's going to be something else. But tonight's proposal is plenty of excitement for one evening.

Drifting off to sleep, I'm wrapped up in a whole lot of love for Maksim and thrilled for what's coming. Our little family is growing, and I can't wait for all the tomorrows we've got ahead of us. Life's just getting started, and it's going to be beautiful.

The End